JANE B.

THE DEAD SILENCE

© 2017 JANE B.

Cover, Illustrations: JANE B.

Editing: Book editing Services

Publisher: Tredition

ISBN

978-3-7439-3709-3 (Paperback)

978-3-7439-3710-9 (Hardcover)

978-3-7439-3711-6 (eBook)

"Again I looked and saw all the oppression that was taking place under the sun: I saw the tears of the oppressed—and they have no comforter; power was on the side of their oppressors—and they have no comforter."

—Ecclesiastes, *4:1*

"Mrs. Sammerson? Mrs. Sammerson, where are you?" the housekeeper called out, prowling among the bushes in the backyard garden of a huge house, her old-fashioned skirt touching the just-blooming peonies with the family of wild bees actively buzzing and working.

The month of May had turned out especially warm and humid. The rain lavishly showered the fertile, prosperous land. The garden breathed with the fragrance of blossoming fruit trees and blooming spring flowers. The trees whispered to each other, discussing last night's storm and its impact, regretting that the ancient oak had not lived through the night. Once a stately giant, the oldest tree had been rotten at its roots. For a long time, this oak had served as a cozy home for the local songbirds, safely sheltering them from the weather and its changeable, moody winds.

Loggers, who had been invited due to the storm, were late, and the housekeeper had to take a detour through the overgrown paths. The main walkway, paved with garden tiles the color of wet river stone, was blocked by the newly fallen tree.

"Mrs. Sammerson, it's time to feed the babe and put her to sleep." The housekeeper frowned. *What could have brought her here, alone, and with the babe?* "It's

5

so slippery, so wet, God only knows whether all the branches had to fall from the tops; otherwise, they could fall on to a restless head," she suddenly crowed through the thickets of wild roses that had chosen an abandoned part of the garden, just before discerning her mistress.

Her mistress's hair, carefully arranged that morning, was messed. Her morning gown, embroidered with gold thread around the edges, was carelessly thrown over a nightshirt tattered in several places. She was not crying, just sitting, leaning forward, immobile, as if her body was frozen. Her chapped lips were trembling, and her hands clutched a crumpled baby blanket.

The housekeeper found her sitting on the edge of the well—a black hole ringed with masonry, like an unhealed wound on the newly rejuvenated body reminiscent of the old, long-gone times, dividing the garden into two parts. It was supposed to have been filled up long ago, but no one ever found the time to do so. First, there had been the death of the old lord (the father of the young mistress); then her quick wedding with a young, promising doctor of psychiatry; and finally the long-awaited birth of their first child. The well had been completely forgotten—until that day.

Her voice was hoarse, but she was not in a hurry to clear her throat, as though she was talking to herself.

"I—I—I just wanted to drink some water. She—she slipped out from my hands. Oh, God, how come?" Finally, the woman burst into tears.

"Mrs. Sammerson, what happened? Lilly. Where is Lilly?"

The housekeeper, perplexed, looked around, trying to figure out where Mrs. Sammerson could have put the poor child. But it was all for nothing. There was nothing on the wet ground except the broken brushwood and leaves of trees surrounding the tragic site.

"Over here." Her mistress pointed to the black circle of the well. There was a small, pale spot on the surface of the dark water.

A note was found in the Mrs. Sammerson's room the next morning:

"Nothing is redeemed. She needs me. I have to be a good mother. I have to be there for her. Forgive me please, my dear Anri. Good-bye. I love you. Forever yours, Angelika."

The body of Mrs. Sammerson was found in the same well where her six-month-old daughter had drowned the day before.

1

"What is the silence?" Anna has raised her eyes and looked at Dr. Sam Haley briefly before looking away, once again inner-focused.

"Perhaps this is death. Perhaps death is the silence … and the darkness … the endless darkness and the endless silence."

The "soul's doctor," Sam Haley turned the page of his notepad and the paper rustled loudly. Anna paid no attention to it.

"Imagine, that there are no sounds at all. No sound of your own heart beating, no breaths." Anna had a light in her eyes, but that was a glassy light with no feelings and no emotions, just a cold, glassy light. "The silence with no life—the dead silence." Anna paused; it seemed to last an eternity.

Sam continued to write something in his notebook. Anna interrupted the stillness.

"Sometimes I want to hear this particular kind of silence"

"Why?" Finally, Sam interrupted her. He raised his head, leaving whatever he was writing, and tried to observe closely Anna's eyes, to understand what she was thinking about. Had she just shared her thoughts or could this conversation could be a hint of a suicidal mood?

From the beginning, Anna appeared as a mystery for him from both sides—professional and personal. Sometimes she humbled him under her stony gaze. He caught himself thinking this was extremely unprofessional and unacceptable from his end. He knew she needed help but was hesitant to offer his own, for reasons he could not understand. Sam did not understand why he was so indecisive next to her. He reverently listened to every word she said, trying to absorb her feelings, but he couldn't understand what was happening to—although he saw obvious progress since their first meeting. At least Anna had started to speak. At the beginning, it was extremely hard for him to pull a meaningful sentence out of her mouth. But now, she spoke to him, every time more and more, opening the door to the dark depths of her morbid mind.

Anna stared into the distance for couple of minutes, as if she were trying to hear the silence, and finally said in a near whisper, "A single second could be enough for me to understand the whole horror and the whole beauty of this kind of silence. I might even

8

feel its coldness." She raised her eyes and a strange smile touched the edges of her lips and immediately disappeared. "For some reason, it seems to me that this silence must be cold." Anna stopped speaking and fell back to her thoughts again.

The doctor broke the silence. "How is your baby doing?" He spoke slowly. Then, quietly, as if afraid to frighten away the wild animals lurking around them, he asked, "You still do not want to tell me either a name or a gender?"

"Name ... baby ... nothing matters. I hear a scream and this scream drives me crazy."

Her voice flashed a hint of some anger and disappeared quickly, returning to its former monotone. "I have to be a good mother. I have to take care. This baby is all that I have." She was talking to herself: every word sounded as if spoken by rote. The voice was becoming more and more saturated with a metallic tone, like the sound on an old record.

"Screams every night, and I can't calm it down ... I can't help—"

"And how do you deal with it during a day? Does the child cry during the daytime?" The doctor did not give up. After all their meetings, he still hadn't gotten a clear story of her child. She never said a name, never used pronouns, so Sam didn't know if it was a boy or a girl. Also, it was hard for him to determine whether Anna was keeping a secret on purpose or if it was just the influence of her disease.

"Daytime?" Anna asked herself. "Daytime ... day ... day ... I don't know ... Mom ... Mom coming soon..." Anna continued to mutter. "Mom, and it will become easier … day … day … a new day. Everything will change soon...."

The clock tinkled out 2:00 p.m. The doctor made another note in his notebook and looked toward Anna but avoided meeting her eyes.

"We have to be done for today. Would you mind coming one more time this week? I would like to talk in more detail about the silence. I think the silence … might be important… Never mind. Could you please make an appointment with my assistant for any convenient time? Have a good one, Anna. See you soon." Sam smiled gently and hurried to his desk, stealing a glance at her eyes.

He liked her eyes, beautiful, deep, and sad. He wanted to drown in her eyes and never come back to the tedious surface of reality, but he could only dip in a little every time when he managed to break through the cold, glassy wall of her impassive gaze. In the rare moments when it seemed to him she felt better, he experienced a strange pleasure in meeting her eyes, despite the fact that her gaze was filled with more than just an easy sadness. Under the touch of banal sadness, the doctor was able to see hints of desperation that had settled in her soul long ago and did not want to leave their cozy shelter.

Sam tried to sort out her problem, tried to understand, but Anna was like an apparition for him, like a ghost gliding between two worlds: the real world with real people and their daily problems and stresses and the world of morbid reveries with its dreadful, horrible apparitions and a dull whisper of a million souls failing to find peace. Sometimes Sam was caught himself, thinking that it would be good to know Anna a little better, maybe the glass wall could crack and slowly began to crumble, giving him the opportunity to learn about her regular life, but only if she weren't one of his patients and so sick. He pitied her, never charged a penny for counseling, attributing his charity to his research. Even though he knew he could get in trouble, Sam didn't want to give up on her. Sam invested all his heart in Anna. Every meeting filled him with more and more doubts about the disease he diagnosed and the therapy he assigned.

"Yes, sure, the silence… Is it important?" Anna asked herself. "I will come … thank you, Doctor." She left the office, carefully closed the door and headed to the reception desk.

"And don't forget to close the window when you leave. It's going to be stormy today. Wait a second, can you wait, yeah, wait."

Gina, Dr. Haley's assistant, was talking on the phone with her new boyfriend—the third one for current year. She wasn't picky about men, probably because of her unshowy appearance and not very sharp brain. But Gina was quite happy even though she was 36 and never married, with no children. Gina was dark-haired and short, and her always slightly disheveled hair had faded long ago, so she had to get it colored at least twice a month to not look like a mangy little monkey. Her nose was a little snub, but pretty nice, and served as the main adornment of her face. A small black mole just below the outer corner of her right eye gave her face a slight piquancy. Her unskillful makeup neither accented nor concealed anything. She never suffered from extra weight, and she was tolerably dressed, not having the willingness and ability to follow the current fashion.

"As usual for Tuesday, 1:00 p.m., Anna?" Gina turned to Anna, briefly interrupting her phone conversation.

"Friday. The doctor wants to see me one more time this week. What about Friday afternoon, as late as possible? I don't want to excuse from work." Anna was standing next to Gina's desk, wrapped in her dark gray jacket, her head down, watching the gray ripples of carpet.

"Friday 4:30 p.m. is the latest available. Would that work for you?"

Sam once made a note to Gina that Anna was a special patient and should be treated differently than all others. Gina didn't pay attention since she didn't care much. She was just doing her job and never asked Sam any extra questions.

"Yeah, thanks. See you on Friday." Anna nodded politely, tried to squeeze out a semblance of a smile, and without raising her head, moved toward the exit. "Silence. This is important," she muttered under her breath while keeping her eyes on the floor.

Anna was lowly, but always clean and simply dressed, medium height, blonde hair, cute. One could even say beautiful. She didn't wear makeup usually, but when she had a few times, she turned gorgeous, catching not only lustful men's eyes, but envious women's as well. Anna tried not to attract any attention, but she still looked strange wrapped up in a warm cloak or jacket and often wearing a hat she forgot to take off inside.

Once she stepped to the elevator in the hall, Anna found herself holding a small figure, the one she was twirling in her hands during the session. One of those ugly figurines that filled a few shelves of one of the cabinets in the doctor's office.

Sam had never pretended to have good taste in collecting all sorts of small, useless things to fill up his spacious office. He got the weird figurines from his aunt as a gift for the last Thanksgiving. She used to give something useful for a household, never giving up on Sam becoming a family guy, but for the last Thanksgiving she brought out the set of figurines.

Not more than four inches high, ceramic, covered with a smooth paint of a dark green-gray dirty color, the figurines pretended to look like animals—the awkward, frightening ones usually pictured in drawings made by kids. The figurine Anna had in her hands looked either like a dog with a bone or a rabbit. The figurine had a rabbit's ears, bulldog's face, and hound's paws too thin and long for such a heavy body. If this animal existed, it would be unable to move, its legs breaking under the heavy weight of its body and head. But luckily it was just someone's imagination. It seemed to Anna that she had seen this animal before, perhaps in a dream.

She put the figurine in her handbag and pushed the elevator button. She decided to return the figurine secretly to its place in the cabinet the next Friday. The elevator doors opened and a trimly clad older woman came out. She politely nodded to Anna and proceeded

13

to the doctor's waiting room. Anna, for some time lost in the depths of her mind, winced and tried to respond with a smile. The woman already had disappeared into the waiting room while Anna was still standing between the elevator doors. Finally, she came around and got into the elevator, letting the doors close.

Anna left the building and headed to the parking lot around the corner. She walked slowly in order not to miss her car. Anna had not gotten used to her new vehicle. Her old Ford Laser made in 1986 had finally abandoned its duties and retired, so she had to purchase another car, a little less old and still ready for a daily routine. Anna remembered she had parked somewhere in the third row from the office center, but had no idea where exactly. Since the car was quite old and cheap, no one had cared to install an electronic lock. Finally, Anna found her 1999 Ford Focus, an unsightly gray color with a scratched right door. It took her a minute to find the keys in her bag, which she then pulled out and dropped on the ground. The keys plopped on the hot pavement with a clanking sound. Anna bent down to pick them up and unexpectedly felt dizzy.

She sat down on the curb next to her car, leaned on her bent knees, and put her head in her hands. It seemed to her that her body ran a light fever. Anna sat there for a few minutes, then gathering her strength, got up and opened the car. Once inside, she relaxed a bit. She felt most calm and safe being alone, away from prying eyes. After her breath recovered, she turned the ignition key. Anna had to get back to work on time.

The way from the doctor's office to Anna's work usually took around 15 minutes. She drove through the quiet streets hidden among the mature trees of an old part of the city center. Passing by houses, Anna looked at the expensive homes, imagining the life of their inhabitants. Here was the father coming home from his job, parking his luxury car in the attached garage, and the whole family out in the hall to meet their dear daddy. His wife was dressed up as if for event, even spending all her time at home. She always looked as if she were going out. Of course, there were a couple of restless pledges of love of the both solicitous parents. They were all beautiful, tidy, well-dressed, and certainly happy. The whole house smelled of delicious food and just baked apple pie. Children interrupted each other trying to tell their father about today's achievements in academics and sports. Anna was always thinking that children who live in such houses should be perfect. They should have enough time for everything: sports and music and also, they could draw beautiful pictures and compose poems that could be performed during family events so their parents could be proud of them.

Anna was sure that world famous sports champions and geniuses were born and grew up in such homes, in such ideal families, and then, when they reached their heights, settled down to have similar miracle families. It seemed to Anna that the world of happiness was a different world, existing so close and at the same time so far away—like a parallel reality. As she passed by the expensive homes, she dreamed about experiencing that feeling of boundless happiness and serenity just once. She wanted at least for a few moments to become one of those happy mothers of a perfect family, waiting for her beloved husband at the doorstep, feeling the warmth and peace of mind of being loved and protected. But the road was rapidly taking her away from the land of dreams and Anna had to get back to reality, every time feeling the acrid bitterness of hopelessness.

2

"Shut up! What else do you need? Shut the hell up! How much longer can you scream?"

The hysterical woman's scream impaled the air in the room, but it was lost against the background of a crying baby. The baby had been crying almost an hour, and the cry became more like a hoarse roar. It seemed that the voices jingled, echoing the walls of the half-empty bedroom. Either the neighbors displayed amazing patience or they just not did not wish to take other people's problems on their own shoulders.

"What do you want?! Are you putting me on?" The woman screamed with uncontrollable rage. Suddenly, she changed her tone to a loving one. "Okay, let me feed you, my dear. Look, here we go, here is your bottle. Come on. Eat some. Come on. We didn't eat for a while."

Her patience did not last long. She roughly grabbed the child with her trembling hands and tried to feed him, but the baby refused to eat and continued to cry. The child's face became redder. There were no tears, just a deaf infant cry that had been rupturing the small weak body.

She dropped the baby on the bed and went out of the room. A little later, she calmed down and came back. She took the baby in her arms, hugged it, and broke into tears. She tried to share all her maternal warmth with the baby, who felt it and began calming down.

"Here we go. See? It's okay. You must be just hungry. Let's eat."

She tried to feed the baby with formula one more time and was lucky with this attempt. The little wrapped bundle opened a tiny mouth and began to suck the milk, gradually falling asleep. She carefully laid the baby in the crib. Her hands were still trembling and tears hadn't dried yet. She stayed without a single motion for a few minutes and almost did not breathe, watching her sweet baby dreaming. Then she smiled and covered the child with a beautiful, half-pink, half-blue baby blanket. Her eyes cleared, her breathing evened out, and the tremors finally left her hands. She sat down on the floor next to the crib and took a deep breath.

The ensuing peace was broken by the impudent invasion. She cried and immediately jumped onto her bed. A huge, black roach had squeezed into the crack between the wall and the window frame and was confidently approaching the changing table. Her body started to shiver. She slowly came down from the bed to the floor, keeping an eye on the uninvited guest. She took a package of baby wipes, managed to jump with a single movement right next to the roach and wacked him with the heavy package of wipes.

After few seconds she caught her breath, pulled out one wipe and grabbed the remains of the monster's body, carefully lifting up the weapon of the recent murder. The woman opened the window and threw the wipe along with the roach body out.

"Get the hell out of here!"

Her eyes gleamed with tears again. She went back to the crib to check on the baby and tuck in the blanket. Tears started to roll down her cheeks. She slid down to the floor between the crib and her bed, her eyes dimmed, and she started to whisper under her breath. "Is this what I was looking for? … Is this what I was dreaming about? I didn't mean … not like this… I didn't… I don't want… I am sorry … forgive me…"

In a few minutes, the whisper switched to a metallic tone. "I have to be a good mother… I have to take care of you… I have to…." The whisper came back. "Oh, Lord… I hate you…"

Tears choked her, not allowing her to utter any words. Soon her regular, quiet voice came back, and turning to the emptiness of the gray color outside the small, dirty window on the opposite wall, she calmly said, "It's okay… I am fine… It's okay…." She was sitting on the floor with her knees folded to her breasts, biting her lips, and swaying slowly. It was cold in the room. Even though she had plugged the holes in the old cracked window frames, the frozen air had found its way into the room and the somber existence of the residents.

The current winter was unusually cold. Too cold for this region. There was no snow, but in the mornings, the small puddles along with the outside stair steps were frozen. Neither she nor the child had any warm clothes.

They both were living through the cold days wrapped in frayed blankets. She did not want to go outside at all. She had enough fresh air inside the apartment. It was hard for her to afford even this tiny, one-bedroom apartment with a small kitchen and living room. It was enough space for them to live, but she often felt she was suffocating in these wet, never dried-out walls. She knew it was harmful for the baby to breathe such air, but this was the best she could do.

The heater turned on loudly and proceeded to make noise until the temperature on the thermostat equaled the temperature in the surrounding air. She had to wrap the thermostat to warm it up and not use too much electricity, so the air in the room never reached a comfortable temperature. She had gotten used to the noise, and it did not bother her a lot. She looked at the clock on the wall. It was late at night. She had to sleep at least a couple of hours, as long as the baby was sleeping. The child would wake up soon and would ask for food again. This thought was jamming her mind. She made the bed, threw her warm cover to the chair next to it, and jumped under the cold blanket.

The thoughts hadn't given her peace of mind. The memories of the bygone days, of the lost dreams and forgotten hopes, drilled her from the inside, leaving the never healed wounds. If it were possible to look at a human soul in the form of a blank sheet of paper, her sheet would be fully pricked with the thick needles of an unruly fate, but despite this, would be still quite clean.

She couldn't manage to fall asleep, turning from one side to the other on the old lumpy mattress. The mattress creaked under the weight of her tiny body. She listened to the breathing of her sleeping child. Slowly her body warmed and relaxed, bringing the messy thoughts along with worrying dreams. She had to be a good mother. She had to…

She needed to rest at least a bit. Tomorrow she would have a lot of work to do. She had to pay for the bills somehow. Finally, her brain gave up and she fell into a deep sleep. The baby, tired after a long-lasting hysteria, had slept through the night.

3

The house of Auntie Darrel, Sam's aunt, was in an area that used to be known as the outskirts of town. The area was clean and quiet, with smoothly mowed lawns around the country-style house facades that had always been brightly decorated for events, especially for the Fourth of July and Christmas holidays.

Dr. Sam Haley—a tall, dark-haired gentleman with beautiful, slightly slanted, brown eyes and an alluring, mysterious, sad smile parked his Mini Cooper off the road because the driveway was busy with a big truck. Sam looked sadly at the old, dark purple sectional around which a few people bustled. He remembered how he, along with his aunt Darrel, went to pick it up at a discount store and how she stuck like a burr to the salesman, asking for the 30-percent discount. The salesman didn't want to agree on anything, but she refused to give up and followed him around, scaring away other potential customers with her sad, almost crying, face. Finally, the salesman gave up and agreed to make a deal with the special discount usually available only to store employees. Auntie was in seventh heaven. Sam could never understand her taste. She did not surprise him at all by picking the dark purple couch, even though the wall in the living room was painted blue. Very rarely he could make a joke about the way she used to dress. She always let it pass, though, since his jokes were never intended to be rude or hurtful, and more than likely, they could be considered compliments. Sam would never allow himself to hurt his aunt who had replaced both his parents immediately after the car accident that divided his life into two parts: before and after. His aunt decided to give up on her own private life and devoted herself to his upbringing. She treasured the memories of her sister, Sam's mother, realizing their importance for the orphaned boy. He was only five years old at the time of the accident, and she was 38. She never had kids of her own. She always dreamed of traveling but had to give up the dream for a while.

Sam approached the house from the garage side, once the home of an old Ford pickup. When he was little, he loved the double cab and roomy outdoor trunk in which his aunt carried paint and tools. She was an artist, earning most of her money by painting the walls in private homes. After Sam became part of her life, she had to get a full-time job with medical insurance, but she also never declined any work on the side, no matter how hard the work was. She remembered how her sister dreamt that her son would grow up and become an outstanding scholar of some science. The main challenge was that she had to be able to give him an opportunity for education, which her family had not been able to afford.

Sam walked into the house, stumbling over the suitcase left on the doorstep. His aunt—an elderly, slightly plump, pretty woman—gave him a few kisses and then sat him down at the table. She put a plate with few pieces of her signature chicken pie in front of him.

"Oh, dear, the pie is especially good this time! Thank you for everything. I can't even imagine how I would manage it alone." Sam was really sorry to part with his aunt.

"Don't overstate the situation." Auntie laughed loudly. "We almost never see each other. You spend all your time at work, and you are not concerned at all about an old dull beggar."

"It's not true, and you know it," Sam interrupted her, proceeding to chew and drop crumbs on his clean pants.

"I won't give up! You need to be able to step over the past and move on. Even from far away. I'll bug you with my hopes. You must let go of the past. For the sake of your future." Auntie smiled widely, walked over and hugged Sam from behind by the shoulders. She then whispered, "Never say never—look how life has turned out. You're not the Lord, although I am sure that he has no final plan for any of us. Everything is in our hands. And your happiness is in your hands." Auntie went back to the stove and poured Sam more hot cocoa.

"My dear, why don't you understand that I am happy!" Sam gave Aunt Darrell an expressive look, but it didn't have the expected effect.

"Of course, *happy*—no one doubts. You just could think about your old aunt. See, I have to get out of here because I can't find anything to do for myself. If

I had a grandchild, I'd never decide on this faraway trip." Auntie waved her hands and sighed deeply.

"I was thinking we are done with that," Sam answered without raising his head. He was busy working on another piece of pie.

"Yeah, we have considered it closed. Why can't it be reopened? Before it's too late." Aunt Darrel stood near the stove, leaning on the kitchen cabinet and did not let up. "And I don't care about the money spent on my ticket, the airlines will reimburse part of the total flight cost."

"Stop whistling Dixie."

"Yes, they will reimburse part. I have checked with them already."

"You wasted your time. We discussed everything long ago."

"Look, it was hard for all of us to go through what happened, but things will straighten out. I won't ever understand you. Even though you don't want to take that risk again, you could at least get married."

"Auntie, please, not now."

"I won't have another chance."

"It seems for the better." Sam smiled. "I hope you know I am kidding."

"Oh, look at this one, another jester. Why didn't you like Tracie? Such a sweet girl and her son is just a wonderful boy." Aunt Darrel rolled her eyes. "You could live, just like anyone else does. At least she could take good care of you."

"I can take care of me myself," Sam answered impassively. Auntie started this conversation every time he visited her. He had gotten used to it and he knew upfront all her possible arguments.

"By the way, she stopped by last night and asked me to say hi to you." Aunt Darrell refused to give up. "She actually liked you."

"Ha, ha, *actually*?" Sam grinned.

"Yeah, she has been a little bit confused with your talking about all these dispossessed and poor people, but in general, she liked you."

"Hmm. Cool. I am glad I still look attractive enough for a "Tracie" kind of woman. It's a pity I can't reciprocate." As usual for any conversation with Aunt Darrell regarding his private life, Sam turned his tone to half-joking.

"Well, of course! You are not interested in regular healthy and wealthy women—you are much more interested in spending your life with the ones you are taking care of.

Auntie was mostly fine with the side projects he was handling besides his job, but it seemed to her that these projects were the cause of his still being single.

"Of course, it's much more interesting," Sam agreed in a half-joking tone. "What do you finding interesting about Tracie?"

"Ha, a lot! She is an individual! She has an expansive personality! You know what I mean!"

"An expansive personality? In your opinion, what makes her that way?"

"Well, she is just like that!"

"Just like that? This is interesting. Let us look at her a little more closely."

"Oh, don't start!"

"You started it! So, when I look at Tracie more closely, I don't find someone who is an individual with an expansive personality. Instead, I find her as an

24

absolute mediocrity, not able to make a simple decision by herself. Even choosing a brand of water to buy— water, just freaking water! Even on this matter, she was looking for 'professional' advice."

"And, what is wrong with that? She is just trying to give her son the best she can."

"What does that mean for a child? Do you really think he cares what kind of water he drinks? Or what color his shorts are? Maybe he is excited about how his uncomfortable cap squeezes his little head all through that ill-fated dinner."

"Quite a nice cap. And he looked really cute wearing it," Auntie tried to argue.

"I'm not arguing that cap isn't nice when considered by itself. But the unlucky child is forced to wear it at the whim of his loony mother!"

"I thought he was fine—and he behaved just perfectly for his age."

"He was looking at us with such weary, tired eyes. He was waiting for the visit to be finally over, so he could eventually escape from the hated and embarrassing cap. All that he really wanted at that moment was to take that freaking cap off and go out to play in the backyard, rather than sitting like a toy soldier, pretending to be a perfect creature just to please his absurd mother!"

"She is the mother! She knows better than anyone what is good for her child." Auntie was exasperated. "Even though I didn't give you birth to you, I've raised you, and I always knew what was good for you," Auntie said in a wounded tone.

"My dear Aunt Darrel, my sweet Auntie." Sam got up from his chair, went to the old woman, hugged her and kissed her forehead. "We are not talking about you and me now, but if you want to know, I can tell you that I always had a clear understanding of the responsibility that came along with raising me, and I was doing my best to bother you as little as I could."

"Yes." Auntie almost shed a tear. "You've always been a good boy. I'm so glad I have you, oh Lord, I don't mean I am glad that my sister is dead, you know. I certainly couldn't give you all the best, but I swear to God, I did my best. I—" She stumbled and decided not to continue. She felt a lump in throat strangling her, preventing her from speaking a word.

"I understand. Don't worry so much. It's okay." Sam leaned over slightly and looked into his aunt's eyes. "I love you so much, and I am thankful for every single minute you've carved out for me. And by the way, I am glad we never had a lot of money and could not afford some things. Sometimes worse is better."

"I don't know, maybe you are right." Auntie gathered herself together and smiled. "You are the doctor here. You know better."

"Okay, let us stop arguing with each other. Let's just talk about something nice and easy."

"Yeah, you are right. It's not the best time for finding out who is right and who is wrong. All right, finish your meal. I'll wrap the leftover pie for you to go." Auntie Darrel took the foil and carefully wrapped the rest of the last pie she had made for her boy. "Whatever happens, you always can join us."

"Life at a resort, as an endless vacation? Pretty attractive, but I am not ready for a rest." Sam took a sip of the cooling cocoa and diligently ate all the crumbs left on his plate. "I could take you to the airport myself, if you want."

"Don't worry, my dear. Frank will give me a ride. We have a lot to talk about on the way, and Minnie wants to see him. I don't mind. He is having a good effect on her." She broke into a broad smile, but her eyes were full of sadness.

Auntie felt a deep sorrow—not for the reason of leaving (and most likely forever), but more about the past, about the things that were happening and would never happen again. She loved this little house, her small kitchen, her cozy living room (even though it was ridiculously decorated), and her neighbors—most of them had been living here since they'd been kids, just like her. The neighbors also loved her for her kindly overbearing simplicity and her inexhaustible, vital energy that she was always open-handedly sharing with anyone who ever felt the need.

Aunt Darrel loved this city as much as this once little boy, and now respectable man, who became a doctor of psychiatry. And now she didn't want to bother him, having decided to spend the rest of her life at the paradise island named Goa, southwest of India, along with her best friend Minnie and a group of "independent," but in fact just lonely, old people. She was facing a long flight and then a cushy life on the sandy beach of the Arabian Sea. Who knows, maybe the doctor would join her eventually, though it was highly improbable.

"Well, I have to go." Sam got up from the table, shook the crumbs from his slightly rumpled pants, took the carefully wrapped leftovers from Auntie's hands, hugged her, and went to the door.

"I can't believe I am saying goodbye." He turned, slightly bowed his head, and said softly, "I love you."

"I love you too, my little man." She walked over to him, gently kissed his forehead and smiled, dashing away the treacherous tear from her cheek. "All right, you have to go, or you'll be late."

Sam had left the house where he grew up, thinking he would not come back ever again. He felt uncomfortable. The gnawing feeling of the impending misfortune gave him no rest for a few days in a row, but Sam could not understand its nature. He had just left the only family he had, and he knew that was forever, but not this thing that was tormenting his soul. He was firmly convinced that Auntie would be fine. He was even glad that she was finally ready to let go and break away from obligations to regain the flexibility of independence and freedom, to fulfill the dream left behind more than 30 years ago for the sake of Sam and to go far away in order to never return home.

All that was cherished by her heart and memory fit into the small, old-fashioned suitcase. She had bought it a few days before grief had befallen their family. She was supposed to journey around the world with her boyfriend, who swore his love and allegiance forever, and who easily went up the ramp and left Aunt Darrell alone with her miseries and a mountain of problems dropped from the skies on her weak shoulders along with unexpected parenthood.

Aunt Darrel had never had any doubts about the choice she made. She loved Sam as if he were her own son and did her best to fill the emptiness in his heart after he lost both parents—or at least as much as possible. Despite his early age, Sam had a clear understanding of how hard it was for his auntie to take care of him. He tried to help her in everything, from the banal dishwashing and housecleaning to the attempts to make some money.

Sam took on any job, but never forgot about the studying. His daily routine until the end of high school was always the same. After school, he jumped from the school bus steps and rushed headlong home. He first finished his homework, then had lunch with whatever he could find in the fridge, and then hurried to make some money.

The neighbors felt sorry for the orphan child and were always trying to find something for him to do, if not in their houses, then by recommending him to their friends. Sam was always busy: someone needed him to mow the lawn, someone needed him to clean up the garbage from the backyard, and someone needed him to go to the store for an extra gallon of milk. Sam was never late and showed respect to his employers, which was highly appreciated, so they invited him again and again, giving him the opportunity to make an extra dime.

Sam gave all the money he made to Aunt Darrel. Every evening, he busily shook out his pockets, smiling proudly. Aunt Darrel deposited all his money in a special savings account to save for his education. She also added to it with any extra dollars she managed to save.

Every evening after coming back from side work, Sam usually shared with Auntie the impressions, feelings, and emotions he experienced during the day. They both sat on the porch with mugs of hot cocoa and talked about anything that came into their minds. As he grew older, Sam started to ask questions that were increasingly difficult for Aunt Darrel to answer, but she did not hand over the position of a competent companion and often secretly read books about the things Sam was interested in at that moment. She was always able to answer him, whatever he was looking for. And Sam listened with interest to Auntie's stories, which she retold in her own manner.

This was how the years went, one after another. Sam grew up, changing his interests and preferences, breaking up with the old friends and finding new ones, falling in love with women his age and older, though he had little success with either in spite of his good looks. As a result of failures and resounding fiascos, Sam had finally decided to concentrate on study and work, but still he could not determine the profession he would like to pursue.

He always had wanted to help people. He wanted to save lives and was thinking about surgery or emergency care. Sam had always stopped himself before speaking out loud, but his aunt knew the thing he wanted to say. If the emergency medical technician who arrived first at the accident had been better qualified, he could recognize the inner injury and avoid the bleeding out that caused Sam's mother's death, and she could have had a chance to survive—but that hadn't happened, and it took Sam a long time to accept it.

His time in school was flying by fast and soon he would have to make a decision. The only thing Sam was sure about was that he wanted to be a doctor, and he put great effort toward going to college. His aunt had saved enough money to cover his future education by combining her everyday savings with the money she got from selling her sister's property as her own part of the modest inheritance left by their parents.

However, neither during his studies in college nor later in medical school could he decide on a specialization until a tragic incident involving one of the students forced him to think about how it is often possible to prevent trouble before it happens. To save lives does not always mean to wait till disaster has come and death is standing behind the magician doctor with her bony fingers crossed.

The suicide of one of the best third-years students at one of the best medical colleges made an indelible impression on Sam, and he finally decided on a specialization, eventually becoming a psychiatrist.

After a few years, Aunt Darrel's face lit with pleasure when she crossed the threshold of the office of the certified doctor of psychiatry, Sam Haley, her adorable nephew and reputable professional. Dr. Haley had spent a little longer in his residency in order to focus more deeply on his chosen specialty. He was happy to adopt the best practices of his senior colleagues and listened to their advice and opinions, respectfully taking into consideration even the most absurd theories. He never tried to stand out at school reunions; instead, he preferred to stand aside and listen.

His skill in listening was his hallmark, and his colleagues made jokes about him, saying he never had a single problem in choosing his specialization. Sam smiled and never tried to argue. He was fine with his colleagues' opinion. But Sam's private life never matched his successful career. As a genetic carrier of Type A hemophilia, part of his inheritance, he lost hope for a happy family. Sam buried his baby immediately after the birth—doctors diagnosed fatal internal bleeding. Sam's wife refused to believe in reality. She failed and finally died. Sam found salvation only in his work. He could not forgive himself that he allowed her to fail and was not around her when she despaired utterly.

But now all this was far in the past, and Dr. Sam Haley had learned to live over again, every day, collecting the pieces of his own soul by helping people in need.

On the way to the office, Sam, as usual took a detour way through the neighborhoods with cheap, but quite safe and cozy housing. He stopped by the tobacco store, right on his way, turned right on the next traffic light, and parked his Mini Cooper next to the fire hydrant, taking a risk of a ticket, because that was the only available spot, but he was not going to stick around for a long time.

He smoked a cigarette and finally got out of the car and directed his steps to a house on the opposite side of the street, jumping over and around the little puddles that stayed on the road after yesterday's rain, decorating the depressing landscape, mirroring the blue sky with clouds slowly moving overhead and catching the rare, lonely bird passing by.

Eric, a cute 10-year-old, shifted from foot to foot on the doorstep of the apartment, hesitating to knock, when the doctor stopped in front. Sam noticed the shoes that Eric was wearing: a brand-new leather pair, leather, still shiny with shoelaces fastened nicely. *Things are getting better*, the doctor thought, and smiled. Then he went to the boy and patted his head.

32

"Well, you got an F again?" Sam smiled in a fatherly way.

"Yeah," said the boy apologetically. "Our math teacher refused to listen to my excuses, but I truly had been helping my mom last night. She is going to be so upset about it." He sighed and casually looked at his new shoes, waiting for the doctor to finally notice and say something about them.

Sam followed his gaze and decided not to disappoint Eric. "Cool shoes!" Sam's face showed true delight. "Brand new! Fit perfectly? No rubbing?"

"Yeah! Brand new!" Eric exclaimed. "Brand new! I chose them myself. And mom bought them for me. I even have a box, and the sales guy gave me a guarantee for 30 days! If anything happens to these shoes within 30 days, I can bring them back and they will exchange them for a new pair." Eric bounced on the balls of his feet. Brand new shoes! Eric had been dreaming about them for a long time while wearing Goodwill donations, the only gifts his mother could afford for her son. But now Eric was absolutely happy wearing his brand-new shoes. For him and his mother that meant the start of their new, better life. Now everything would change and no one would ever laugh at him at school. They wouldn't call him "junkman" anymore.

Sam could not help but remember his own deprived childhood. He was also teased at school because he wore old donated clothes, saving each penny for education, not able to afford anything new. He got his first brand-new suit upon graduating high school when Auntie Darrel estimated all the education costs and realized they had enough already. He never had any grievance. She did the right thing, and now he could rejoice together with this simple-minded little boy, being able to understand his happiness in full.

"I am so happy for you!" Sam patted Eric's shoulder.

"Yes, but the whole picture is spoiled by my F. Mom tries her best, and I failed."

"It's okay. The main thing is knowing that you are right. Who cares about the grades? Let's go. I'll talk to your mom."

"Thank you, my friend!" Eric livened up and knocked on the door without any delay.

After a minute, the door opened. Eric's mother—a woman who had a child after 40—met both with a smile. "Dr. Haley! Hi, I am so glad to see you! Hey, Eric, you are late. Did anything happen?" She helped her son take off his heavy school bag. "Are you okay?"

"Yes, Mom, I'm fine." The boy dropped his eyes, sat down on the ottoman next to the door and began slowly unlacing his shoes. "Don't worry, okay. I'll fix my F. This teacher, you know, she just doesn't like me. Every time she bugs me." He finally had his shoes off and lifted up his head.

"Don't worry, my dear. I'm not upset. I know for sure you are smart! Go wash your hands, and we'll have lunch." She hugged Eric and sent him to the bathroom, lightly slapping his back.

Eric did not go to the bathroom immediately. First, he took the shoebox out of the closet, gently laid his shoes in it, and put the box back. Than he ran to the bathroom while singing some funny song.

"Dr., please join us."

"Oh, thank you, Ali. I just left my auntie, by the way. Here is some of her best chicken pie." He handed her the wrapped pie. "Enjoy it." Then he paused and asked, "Ali, are you all right? How do you feel? Do you need any help?"

"Oh, thank you, Sam. You are so kind to us." She tried to hide her embarrassment but welled up with tears. "We are fine, thank you."

"How is your new job? Are they paying well enough?"

"Oh, Yes, yes! All is good! I was offered a new position with full health insurance, a 401(k), and some other benefits. I am starting next week. I will do my best and work hard at the beginning, but I can handle it, I am sure." Ali's voice was full of hope and confidence. "The only thing is, I'll have a little less time to spend with Eric, but he understands everything and helps me a lot. I think you noticed his brand-new shoes. He is so happy having them."

"He is a good boy. You should be proud of him."

"Yes, he is doing his best. Thank you for everything, Dr." Ali walked over to Sam and hugged him. "I've been wanting to tell you. I am sure you know it ... well ... if you hadn't stepped up, at that moment, you know..." Her eyes began to tear. "I could ... we could ... have failed."

"Don't say that, Ali, not at all. I am a doctor. I must help people." Sam smiled and found himself a little embarrassed.

"Now we are really doing well. And soon, I won't even need to work late nights any more, as we will have enough to live on. And by the way, I am trying to save some to, you know, pay you back what I owe."

"Ali, there is no debt. It's okay. I will forget everything on one condition." Sam smiled conspiratorially.

Ali's eyes flashed a question. "What kind of condition?"

"Promise me that you'll be happy."

Ali gave up and the tears ran down her face.

"I have to go." Sam hugged her. "I might be leaving town soon. So, I am really glad that you are okay. But if anything happens, Ali, I will leave you my cellphone number and my address. Let me know, anytime, please, no hesitation. It's my job to help, so please, I am asking you now, if anything happens, let me know immediately—not for yourself, but for him." Sam pointed to the bathroom door.

"Yes, be sure. I would never ever … I … Now I can handle it."

Eric ran out of the bathroom, jumped to the doctor, and pulled his sleeve.

"Let's go eat! I'm so hungry"

Sam hugged the boy and whispered in his ear, "You know my phone number. Whatever happens, I will be always here to help you and your mom. Don't forget, you are not alone. You are doing a great job! Regarding your math teacher, don't pay too much attention to her. I guess no one loved her when she was a child and she is just jealous that you have such a great mom and that she really loves you so much. This is the most important thing. And remember, never give up!" Sam straightened. "I have to go." He smiled and walked out the door, thinking to himself that he would miss these two. But they were fine now and able to live without him. There were too many other people who needed his help, and it was time to move on.

Sam returned to his car, playfully jumping over the puddles encountered on his way. He turned the ignition key, lit a cigarette, and drove off. After touring several homes of his voluntary mentees, which is how he referred to people he helped, he finally went to his office.

He had simple logic. Since he could not have children, but really loved them very much, Sam decided to split his life into two parts. The first part—his job—he was doing for money. The second part—the major part of his life—he was helping families who found themselves in difficult situations. As a rule, it was single-parent families, mostly mothers, who, for whatever reasons, have been left alone with the children and alone with a world full of misfortunes.

Sam had decided that he didn't need a lot for himself, and anyway at the end, when going to the other side, he wouldn't be taking anything with him. He wasn't expecting any heir to appear; he was fine with his small apartment and had enough money for his own daily expenses. The rest he spent helping others buying food, renting apartments, and getting them paid for a few months in advance—this way he was giving a single parent some time to get out of a difficult situation. He also helped them find a job and decent, affordable daycare and schools for their children.

He was doing everything to help them get their lives out of the way of destruction, and as soon as he saw the situation getting better and they were able to handle it, he left them on their own to proceed with their lives, but with new strength, hope, and much more confidence. To put it simply, Sam was a kind of a guardian angel for many kids and their families caught in unexpected troubles.

Dr. Haley did not like to go out; he'd never been attracted by the nightlife of the big city or a meaningless, drunk conversation with vulgar jokes and often just outright stupidity. He was completely submerged in his work. He had his for-profit patients during regular working hours, and the rest of the time, besides his "helping projects," he had his research on mental disorders associated with children's invisible— as he called them—injuries.

Sam slept little, and when he did, it was a kind of broken sleep. He went over and over the experiences of his mentees, imagining the many different ways an injury to a child's mind can develop and affect his or her adolescence, hoping to minimize if not nullify the damage. However, Sam had a strong constitution and was always full of energy to proceed, even if he had no sleep for a few days in a row. His office was his second home where he spent most of his time, escaping from thoughts about his past and hopes about his future.

4

"You scratched me again!" A disgruntled female voice sounded loudly. She grabbed the mirror and stared at her reflection, eyeing the fresh scratch on her right cheek near the nose.

"What if I scratched your face? Would you like that?"

Flinging the mirror on the bed, she went to the child who was sitting on the floor, surrounded by a few toys: crooked short haircut, faded clothes, and unwashed face with big, twinkling eyes. The child looked frightened but did not dare to cry, pushing the lump in the throat back down, afraid to move. The woman grabbed the child by the shoulders and began to shake. The child continued to keep silent and looked at the mother with scared eyes. It looked like the child had not found anything unusual in the mother's attitude, but the child still was scared.

The mother's anger was abruptly replaced with humility. Her gaze ran around the room for a few seconds; then, she let go of the baby's shoulders and sat on the floor staring at one point.

"This is all my fault. Me, only me, who is a failure. Nothing to do with you. This is only me. I am a bad mother." The woman started to cry, but suddenly, she calmed down and said with a strange smile, "It's time to make nails. Let's cut them off."

She put the child into the crib and left the room. She found the scissors in the kitchen and came back to the baby's crib. The child sat huddled in the corner of the crib and nervously fingered the sleeve of a shirt. She bent over, took the baby out of the crib and had the child sit down on the changing table. The child did not try to resist or move. If not for the breathing and frequently twinkling eyes with a scared gaze, the child might be a well-made doll rather than something alive.

"Don't move"

The tone of the women changed again, her voice sounding cold and indifferent. Her eyes became filmy.

"Don't you dare move!" Her eyes became wide and bloodshot. "Otherwise I'll hurt you, painful, very painful. Just like you did! Like you hurt me! It hurts!"

Her hands were shaking. The child was silent. The baby's little body was trembling with fear. It was so usual for the child to feel fear. Just as usual as feeling hunger or cold.

"Here we go. Careful, I'll show you how to hurt me. I will not allow anyone to hurt me ever again. You won't scratch me anymore. We will fix it. I promise."

With trembling fingers, she grabbed the child's chubby little hand and tried to cut the nails on the fingers of the left hand. The child suddenly jerked, angering the mother as though she had been hit on the head. She shivered, sharply seized the baby's hand and pressed the scissors with all her strength.

Her gaze was glued to the wall; she didn't even look at the child at that moment. She was in another space, she was absent, but her fingers continued to hold the baby's arm and forcefully pressed the scissors.

It was a piercing scream, choking in pain, a helpless scream—the wild eyes were filled with fear, questioning only one thing: "Why, Mom?"

The sound of the heart-rending child's scream brought her back to reality. She came around and was stunned by the nightmarish picture. The kid was lying on the changing table and crying. Everything nearby was covered with blood; the child alternately was screaming and choking from the pain and horror.

She dropped the scissors from her hands and could not understand who had hurt her baby. Realizing the full horror of what she had done, in a panic she grabbed the child and ran into the bathroom, washed the wounds and then went to the kitchen, put the child on the cold floor, and tried to find some antiseptic. Finally, she found hydrogen peroxide and washed the wounds. The child continued to scream, while the woman cried and could not believe she had hurt her only darling.

After she had treated the wounds with peroxide, she bandaged both chopped fingers and gave the child a strong painkiller prescribed for her long before. She cut a small piece of one pill, crumbled it, and dissolved it in a glass of milk. The medicine started to work soon, and the child calmed down.

She continued crying, quietly and hopelessly. She thought it was a bad dream. She whispered, "Mom, mom will come soon... Mom ... and it would become easier. Mama, mama..."

She calmed down a bit, gathered her courage to enter the bedroom and clean all traces of the recent occurrence. The child fell asleep, and she was cleaned of blood stains, singing a song under her breath:

Sleep, my fine young baby[1]
Lullabye, a-bye.
Quietly the clear moon looks down
Into your cradle
I will tell you stories,
I will sing you a song,
Sleep on, close your eyes,
Lullabye, a-bye.

She had heard this song in her distant, misty childhood, as in another life. After everything was cleaned up, she finally calmed down and decided that such thing would never happen again. It was an

---

[1] Michail Lermontov "Cossack Lullaby"

accident—she didn't want to hurt her child. She loved her child, loved as much as she was able to love. If she was still able, if she still loved.

She had to be a good mother. The child was everything she had.

Fatigue was striking her down. It was late at night. Cold wind howled behind the window. She needed to sleep. She would have to get up early tomorrow, would have to work. She raised the temperature on the thermostat, and the heater started to make a muffled noise. The constant, monotonous sound was soothing her, it seemed. She had stopped hearing her own thoughts. Finally, she fell into a sweaty, morbid sleep.

5

Gina was especially friendly today, which was not surprising since it was Friday, the end of the working week, and of course, she had a bunch of plans for her weekend. Her recent romance had been turning into something more, and Gina could not hide her joy. Despite all the assurances that she was an independent woman, self-sufficient, and not a "half" of someone, she, just like anyone else, had been missing a faithful partner who would accept all her faults and imperfections and would go through life with her.

Secretly she had still been hoping to become a mother. "*It's not a problem in our times. Women are having their first babies after 40, and of course , there is a risk, but the young mothers also have a risk, and at the end, we are all under the will of God.*" Gina thought this way and hoped for the best. Anyone would envy her optimistic nature. After so many failed relationships, she still believed in men and every time jumped into the vortex up to the hilt, just like the first time, sharing all of herself and giving everything she had.

It seemed like her last unfair relationships had exhausted her completely. But no! It took her a month to recover after the last failure and get back to the innumerable army fighting on the battlefield of love all around the world.

Gina had been making a long-term forecast for her previous boyfriend, who had disappeared one rainy morning. He left for the nearby café to get some breakfast and took with him all the valuable jewelry Gina had. She waited for him all day, long refusing to believe he would never come back. She genuinely worried for him, even was about to call the police, but couldn't find any pictures of her boyfriend who was pretending to be her fiancé early the same morning. At first, she persuaded herself that it was her fault that she pushed him too far, and he eventually got scared of their rapidly developing relationship. Gina had read in one magazine that all men are afraid of responsibility and they need time to accept the fact of impending loss of freedom. Gina had calmed herself a little this way, and she decided that he just needed time, maybe a day or two, or maybe a week.

But weeks passed by slowly, one after another, and she did not receive any word from him. Eventually, Gina got mad and decided she was tired of sitting at home and waiting until he deigned to accept the loss of his single status. She put on her best outfit and went out to get a couple of drinks in the same bar where they had met. She was sure she would find him there. When they met there the first time a few months before, it seemed to her that he was a frequenter of that bar. She noticed the bartender talked with him as with an old acquaintance, calling him by name, while the waitress did not wait for him to order—she just brought him his usual picky drink choice.

She pulled on her only pair of high-heeled shoes, made up her face carelessly, and decided to complete her look with her jewelry, which was just a pair of gold rings, a gold brooch, and a thin platinum chain with a small pendant decorated with a tiny diamond in the middle. At that moment, Gina found out that she had been robbed by her ex. The dull pain squeezed her chest like she had been hit, but from the inside. She treasured these lovely things she had inherited from her grandmother, and now they were gone. She finally realized that her ex would not come back. Gina was too ashamed to go to the police and doubted whether they would deal with such a trifle. And how would she prove that she had never given him jewelry, and then, when he had left, decided to take revenge because of jealousy and resentment? The last thing she needed at that moment was to make excuses for her failures in her personal life in front of strangers, and she decided to take everything that happened as a lesson and move on.

She still went to the bar that night to fill up with alcohol her inner wounds and to cry out all her concerns to the stranger at the next seat. She took the only free seat at the end of the bar on the corner, next to the bathroom. Gina was expecting nothing but a morning hangover, and the inconspicuous seat in the corner was just the right place to match her mood.

She had ordered a double extra strong and extra dirty martini with two extra blue cheese olives and sat slowly sipping her drink, looking at clean, glistering glasses huddled at her left. People on the seat next to her changed every few minutes. They sat down for a while, ordered, and after their order was ready, grabbed it and got lost in the recess of the barroom. No one was eager to stay near the toilet.

Gina stopped paying attention to the seat with its rotating guests. Another man sat down on the chair next to Gina and ordered. But after he had gotten his drink, he hadn't budged and hadn't gotten lost in the crowd of the cackling visitors. He remained next to Gina, timidly looking in her direction. She hadn't noticed him right away, being lost in her sad thoughts, regretting the lovely little things dear to her heart that were gone forever, remembering the days when they still belonged to her grandmother.

The man who had been sitting next to Gina noticed that her glass was almost empty and ordered her one more drink with a short sign to the bartender. When the bartender placed a glass with a new portion of martini in front of Gina, she did not realize that it was for her and looked at him confused. The man in the next chair finally found courage and spoke to her.

"I apologize, but I took the liberty to buy you a drink, if you don't mind, of course. I understand if you are angry, but I really am hoping for your kindness."

Gina felt like if she had been splashed with cold water. She came around, returned to Earth from the recesses of her memory, but couldn't find immediately what to answer, being a bit confused and surprised at the same time. The man had noticed her confusion and proceeded to talk.

"Let me introduce myself. My name is Matthew Stevens, and I have a practice in the vet clinic here around the corner. Today was a hard day for me. I performed my first surgery on a dog. Actually, it was supposed to be a regular spaying, but during the surgery I found a tumor; thank God it was benign, but nevertheless. Anyway, it was not easy to excise a tumor, and it was the first surgery I did myself. And here I am." He uttered all this with one breath. Then after a short pause, spoke again.

"So, I decided to get a drink, kind of celebrate my first success. But I don't know anyone here, and it seemed to me that you're bored or just sad, so I took the liberty—maybe you would like to celebrate with me? Do I look too stupid?"

While he was talking, Gina had enough time to scan his face, and she felt pretty free to look at him directly and considered that she actually liked him. He seemed to be nice and funny.
Apparently, the man was tall: he was sitting slightly hunched over, with both his hands on the bar counter, but he didn't touch his drink. He had a high forehead, medium-sized nose with a hump, deep-set but expressive gray eyes, thin lips, and red, sparse bristles exactly the same color as his hair.

Gina smiled and answered. "No, I mean, not stupid, and no, I don't mind." She took the offered glass with the new martini. "Cheers, for your success!"

Matthew raised his drink, Gina raised hers, and he lightly touched his glass with hers. "Cheers."

Gina smiled and looked into the eyes of her new friend. Matthew did not shift his eyes. He missed a beat for a second, then he smiled back and they both took a sip of their drinks.

That night they both talked incessantly. Gina forgot about her last failed relationships, and Matthew no longer felt lonely. He walked her home, but being a true gentleman, refused the invitation for coffee. He confined himself to a timid kiss of her cheek, which enraptured Gina since usually all her boyfriends were looking to get a "cup of coffee" at their first date.

But Matthew seemed to be a quite different story. Well mannered, polite and intelligent, sometimes too shy, he looked at her in a different way. Gina felt so warmed when he was looking at her. They exchanged their phone numbers and finished that night alone in their own beds, dreaming about each other.

And tonight, just three months after they had met each other, she was going out to dinner with Matthew's parents. She was a little nervous. This was the second time in her life when her boyfriend was going to introduce her to his parents, and for Gina it was significant event.

6

"Dr. Haley will be a little late. He asked you to wait a bit, please. Take a seat, Anna. May I offer you anything to drink?"

"Yes, please. Hot tea, if you don't mind."

"Sure! Give me a minute." Gina smiled and disappeared into the kitchen.

Anna didn't want tea. She just wanted someone to take care of her a little.

"Thank you, Gina. You look so nice today."

"Oh, thank you, Anna!" Gina had brightened up. "I have spent the whole morning on hair and makeup—even had to get up an hour earlier!" She touched her hair. "Usually I am getting ready pretty quick, 30 minutes is enough for everything, if we don't count breakfast time, but today I spent two hours and did not even have time for breakfast." Gina was speaking fast with a note of delight. She wanted someone to ask her about the reason, even if it would be the patient Gina considered a really sick one because of her strange behavior.

"I bet you have a great reason, don't you?" Anna asked.

"Oh yes! Anna, of course, I have a reason!" Gina was happy with the opportunity to share her news with someone and didn't want to miss it. "My boyfriend persuaded me to be introduced to his parents. I certainly don't think it is the right time and really necessary," Gina fibbed a little, "because we have been dating for only a few months, but he insisted so much that I couldn't say no to him. We are going to have dinner tonight at Sixty, a fancy restaurant located on the sixtieth floor of the Hyatt hotel in midtown. It has such a beautiful view of the city and revolves so you can see the city from different points. I even had to buy a new pair of shoes—I have them here under my desk, and I will put them on right before I go out. And, of course, my dress, I had to bring it to work with me as well, because I would look weird wearing an evening dress since morning."

48

Gina laughed joyfully. She was so busy telling her story that she had not paid attention to Anna, who absolutely was not listening to her and was completely self-absorbed. But Gina frankly didn't care if she had been listened to. She really wanted to speak out and she got her chance. Gina went back to her desk singing a cheerful song.

Anna sat on the couch with biscuits in her hand. She never opened the package and didn't take a single sip of her tea. She had been deeply engrossed in her own thoughts and wasn't paying attention to what was happening around her.

The doctor was 20 minutes late. Apologizing, he went to his office, and two minutes later invited Anna.

"Hello, Anna, please have a seat." The doctor pointed to the lounge seat.

Anna sat down, but first, as usual, she took one of the ugly animal figurines from the cabinet shelf. She imagined that she was talking to the figurine, which made it easier for her to speak since she actually didn't want anybody to hear some of the things she talked about. She thought it would be better to keep some things secret and unspoken, but the clay figurine would not hear and would not judge—it didn't care about anything that had been done.

"You wanted to talk about the silence," Anna said quietly. "I have been thinking about it a lot. I have nothing to say to you. I cannot find words to describe the way I feel."

It seemed to Sam that Anna felt a little better in comparison to their last session. She had a clear gaze, the usual tremor had left her hands, and she looked absolutely calm and mentally normal—or as normal as it is possible to judge about the mental health and normality of a person by her appearance. The doctor took a chance in asking the question that he always wanted to ask, but never had the right moment.

"Let's talk about the baby, or maybe about the father of the child," Sam offered.

Anna's face changed. Her gaze became distracted again. Dr. Haley thought he physically felt the whole heavy weight of the burden Anna had been dragging on her shoulders and could not throw away either herself or with his help. Also, it seemed to him like the body of the woman instantly grew heavy and dark as if it were filled with poisonous juices from her injured mind.

"I love my baby. My baby is all I have," Anna said slowly, steadily, clearly, pronouncing each word carefully.

They were not her words, it was not her voice, the phrase sounded as if it was memorized under pressure or duress. The words sounded so dead and lifeless the doctor lost his last doubts that the baby and everything related to the baby was the most painful matter, and perhaps the main reason Anna had succumbed to the disease.

"The cry turns to a roar. A dull roar, like something is tearing from the inside, wants to come out, but it can't break free. The cry … every night. I don't sleep. I'm so tired." Anna continued to speak in a toneless way and not clearly or distinctly. It took all Sam's attention to understand some of her words.

"Maybe your child feels your condition and it is bothering him. It's not a secret that children reflect their parents' mental mood. Try to calm down and your baby will follow you."

The doctor tried to bring her back to reality, spoke loudly, even stood up from his chair and came closer, trying to get her attention.

"Anna, please try to think, what could appease you? What could bring you pleasure and joy? If you could do just anything, imagine for a moment that you can have one wish, what would you like the most?"

Now Sam's voice sounded soft, as if floating in the air, so gentle and calm, gliding across the room, reaching his patient and wrapping her with its warmth. Anna raised her eyes and looked at the doctor. He was standing close to her; she could hear his troubled breathing and could pick up his smell, and for a moment, it seemed that she was ready to let him get closer, to get to know him better and accept his help, but after a second she changed her mind, turned her eyes to the figurine that was in her hands, and drifted away, diving back into her world. Her hands sweated so much that figurine slipped out and almost fell, but Anna caught it at the last moment and pressed it to her breast. This time it was something that looked more like a horse, but with frog eyes and soft paws instead of hooves. Anna's gaze froze, and she slightly bowed her head to the right, as if trying to see something behind the doctor's back, then frowned and started to speak with the unpleasant, metallic tone in her voice.

"We were making nails, cutting them off." Anna bowed her head more to the right, slightly turned it down and screwed up her eyes. "Hurts. Oh, God, how painful, how ugly. Blood, I hate blood." Then she opened her eyes wide, straightened up, and continued impassively. "It's much better, it's much easier. It will be fine. I will take care of you. I have to take care…"

"Anna, what happened? Have you hurt the baby?" The doctor was alarmed in earnest; he looked at her and tried to understand if she was telling the truth or if this was just a fantasy of her sick mind. "Have you seen the doctor? Have you treated the wounds? Anna, please, it's not a joke."

"It's all right. Baby … that's all I have." Anna repeated the memorized phrase in the same lifeless, unemotional tone.

"Being in such a condition, you can hurt your baby. Please, could you allow me to help you?" The doctor finally managed to offer her his help. "If you … if you don't want me to help you, there are some people … they can help you. Please, Anna, they can help you and your child." Sam tried to look into her eyes, but she did not meet his gaze. She sat motionless, as if shackled; her soul and mind had never known freedom and did not belong to her at that moment.

"Anna, maybe … maybe you could bring your baby to our next session? I could stop by your place and help you, if you don't mind, if you would like…"

"Help … Mom, mama, help … Maria… She loves me…" Anna's lips showed a suspicion of a smile, but her eyes still looked at nowhere.

"Maria? Who is Maria? Is it your mother or a nanny? I remember you told me that you didn't know your mother well enough."

The doctor fell silent, lost in his own thoughts and quickly began to flip through his notebook, trying to find the note about Anna's mother. He knew for sure that he had written some comments regarding this important matter. Anna did not seem to notice him; she spoke to the figurine that was still in her hands.

"Maria … caring…" Anna pressed the figurine to her breast again and tilted her head slightly to the right. "Maria … beautiful name." She turned to the window and spoke under her breath. "If I have a girl, I would name her Maria."

Sam didn't hear and missed those words; he finally managed to find the right note and was making some new notes in his notebook. The scrape of his pencil over the paper sounded louder than Anna speaking.

"Anna, can you tell me about the baby's father? How did you meet him? Does he know that he is a father?" The doctor stared at Anna, trying to catch at least some emotion on her face, but it remained motionless.

"Father?" Anna suddenly raised her head and stared at the doctor. Her face showed concern, as though she was trying to remember something, but that it remained difficult. "I don't know. Father." A faint smile stirred her lips. "I know what kind of person he is." The smile turned into a vicious grimace of disgust. She didn't seem to be talking to the doctor but instead to the figurine in her hands. "Father never wanted to know about the baby! He does not exist!" Unexpectedly, Anna abruptly stood up, walked to the window and leaned forward, slightly touching the cold glass with her forehead and clutching the pulled-up tulle in one hand. In the other hand, she kept rubbing the figurine. She closed her eyes and waited a few minutes, then took a deep breath, and returned to her seat. The doctor decided not to perturb her anymore and left the sore subject.

The rest of the time they talked about different things that seemed to bother Anna as much as family problems. She complained of not being able to wear a short-sleeve blouse to the office because the air conditioning was right above her desk and the cold air was blowing on her constantly, and even in summer she felt cold. So, she could get sick and, God forbid, die from the disease, and so she had to wear warm clothes at all times. She also talked about some serious issues. For example, Anna was extremely worried about recent events in Orlando when an American man of Afghan origin, who reportedly belonged to ISIS, shot people in a gay night club. He killed about 50 people.

"It's so scary, Dr. All these people were the special ones to someone... It hurts so much to lose the children."

For a moment, the doctor thought her glassy gaze returned, but Anna looked straight ahead, sometimes turning her eyes with a clear as a sunny day gaze to the doctor. She returned the figurine to its place on the half-empty shelf, not forgetting about the one borrowed the last time. She carefully pulled it from her bag and placed it among the others.

"So easy—just because someone decided that his opinion is more important, and his way of thinking is the only right way to think. Do you believe in God, Dr.?" Without waiting for his response, Anna continued. "I do believe. But for me, God is the will. The human will and the power of thoughts and actions. Starving people, why wouldn't they get up and start working? Why not demonstrate will and strength? I am not talking about the sick and real invalids. Just regular homeless or beggars or those who complain about their life all the time. It would be worth nothing to change their lives because they have the main thing: They have life. The opportunity to breathe, to see, to hear, and to feel. They are not crippled, well, okay, even if crippled, in our time, this is not a final sentence, there are so many areas where they can find themselves and feel harmony. No education? It's okay. It's not a reason to stoop to begging. You can go and wash the dishes, the floors, clean the streets or do anything else; the world has enough simple work that still needs to be done, but it is easier to be a victim of anything, of the government, circumstances. There are always a lot of excuses that can be found. They are entreating God to help them, to forgive, but all they need to do is to see the God in themselves. To get their shit together and start to move! Not to lose self-confidence, to continue thinking, trying, and to be assured that one day everything will be fine. The main thing is not to give up ever. But this way is too hard because you have to rely on yourself only, you have to make a decision, you have to take responsibility for decisions you've made. It's much easier to entreat, to blame some invisible forces for any failure; it's much easier to blame somebody than to admit your own failure and weakness. It is easier to take someone's opinion as a rule, as an unbreakable axiom that calls you to a certain action." Anna's eyes filled up with rage. "After all, they have a major gift—life."

Anna got up from the lounger and walked over to the cabinet with figurines. She did not need the figurines at that moment; she was talking to the doctor, not hiding and looking into his eyes with her stony gaze.

Sam listened to her with interest, wondering about the difference between Anna who was drowning in the deeps of her morbid mind, and Anna who was speaking about other people's fates and decisions.

Two different persons appeared today in front of him in one face. Sam tried to remember the turning point, the transition between one condition to another in order to understand what brought her there and how to help her avoid these transitions in her routine life. How to help her avoid going deep inside her mind. Anna continued to speak, taking up her usual position on the lounger.

"I mean, I am not too much of a spiritual person, but I do believe. Sometimes I go to church, and I always wear my crucifix." Anna automatically touched the small gold cross that she always wore. "I'm talking about the weaknesses that people consider a true faith. About switching the ideas, prevarication, all these atrocities that people commit, hiding behind faith. The faith in some people's understanding today is a set of canons, indisputable rules, well-built opinion about some certain things, dictated with the consent of the consumer of that faith. That guy in Orlando, he shot people because in his faith's opinion, the faith in its distorted concepts, they did not deserve to live. That's not his opinion, that's the opinion of his faith. His faith has decided for him what is good and what is wrong; the faith was thinking instead of him and took the responsibility that his life has failed, and he was fine with that because all his failures have been explained and excused by some reason, in which the faith, I mean the faith in its distorted concepts, blamed other people. People who have different points of view regarding some things. The faith has turned him against people who are different from us; he capitulated to his faith without any fight. Human weakness, laziness plus the dictated faith, with the answers ready for any question—this is convenient, this is the strongest weapon, the terrible weapon. It will not be the bombs or diseases that will destroy this world. The world will be destroyed by the faith in the way it exists and is presented today. Ignorance has always been the sworn enemy of humankind. It has always thwarted progress, destroying the best. I feel a great regret for all those who have suffered and still are suffering at the hands of the weak, the ignorant, the lazy incompetents."

Anna finished and got up from the couch; her cheeks were burning, but the skin remained its usual pale grayish color.

"The session time was over long ago, wasn't it?" She went over to the door. "See you next Tuesday. Have a good one."

Anna left the doctor's office without saying goodbye to Gina. She disappeared into the elevator hall, accidentally slamming the door so loudly that Gina finally came down from heaven to Earth, jumped from her chair, and ran into Sam's room to ask him if everything was okay. She found Dr. Haley, as usual, sitting at his desk and writing something. He raised his head and was surprised by her scared face.

"Are you okay?" Sam was ahead of Gina with his question.

"Oh, yes, Dr., my apologies. I thought … never mind."

57

Gina slightly smiled and closed the door, leaving the doctor with his usual chores. Sam sat in the office until late that night. Gina left to have dinner with her boyfriend's parents. Dr. Hayley was thinking about Anna; he could not believe that she could hurt her own baby. As far as he managed to get to know her as a patient and as a human being, in his opinion, she was unable to hurt anyone. Anyone, except, of course, herself. Sam couldn't believe that Anna spoke the truth about the baby, or at least he didn't want to believe she did. She had been something more for him, more than just another unhappy, clouded mind lost in life. Maybe he just misunderstood her.

"What did she mean? What's going on with her? I am not the worst doctor. Why can't I break through to her?"

He addressed these questions to Green Joe, the cactus that had been living in the doctor's office, again and again; he could not accept the fact that she was sick and most likely would not ever recover. Green Joe was silent, and Sam had to justify his own non-involvement and inaction. He wasn't in a hurry to give up on Anna, relying on the help of one of his colleagues, an older, respected colleague with whom he became acquainted during his studies at the university.

Sam had been visiting Patrick, the old man, for advice when he was looking for a second opinion and sometimes just to talk and to check on him. Patrick had retired long ago and did not take any patients, but was always happy to advise and support his talented young colleague. He considered Sam a capable budding specialist. Their rare joint dinners were pleasing to the old man, and Patrick tried to help Sam as much as he could. During one of these dinners, Sam shared his doubts about Anna. Patrick listened carefully, but did not hurry to express his opinion. Usually it never took him long to find an answer to any of Sam's questions, but this time he only said that some cases require a special view and wrote down the phone number of Anri Sammerson and advised Sam to contact him. According to Patrick, Professor Sammerson was the one who could not only help Sam figure out Anna's case, but if he got lucky and the professor counted him as competent and credible, he could help Sam with his research.

Sam could not reach the professor right away. It was not that easy since Anri was quite busy and wasn't too familiar with modern means of communication. But Patrick had warned Sam that the professor was old school, preferring personal meetings to any other kind of communication. He didn't trust cellphone or email connections.

Sam tried hard to reach the professor and finally his call was answered. The professor had quite a pleasant voice, though a little hoarse. He cleared his throat and politely introduced himself as Professor Anri Sammerson. Dr. Haley had already gotten used to the fact of his never responding to calls and got lost for a second, but he rapidly got himself together and with a courteous greeting introduced himself as well.

The professor listened to the doctor without interrupting, then asked his full name and contact information, promising to call him back shortly, then he quickly said goodbye and, without waiting for a response, hung up.

Of course, Sam was not expecting much from their phone conversation, but he hoped, at least, that he would get an appointment. Most of all, the doctor did not like the situation to be up in the air, unresolved.

After that phone call, Sam had a strange feeling. He felt like somebody had turned him inside out and forgot to return his guts back to their place; they scattered them around instead. The idea had crept into his mind out of nowhere that everything he knew and was doing made no sense and that nothing was right.

Sam tried to remember what exactly the professor said and at what point he began to doubt, but he did not recall a single unnecessary word. He hadn't heard anything special, just a short greeting, questions about his contact information and a quick farewell. Nothing that could unbalance the doctor's mind.

Sam did not make it home that night. He laid down on the couch and tried to have a therapy session with himself, to feel as a patient would feel, but he didn't dig deep into his mind. He'd had a hard day and sleepiness quickly took over.

Sam woke up the next morning to the sound of vacuuming coming from the reception room. Cleaners were performing their regular morning duties. The doctor, pretending he had just arrived, went to the kitchen to make some coffee. He wondered at his feeling yesterday, but didn't give it much importance, deciding that it was just his fatigue. Distracted by his regular routine, he stopped thinking about the professor.

A few weeks passed. Patients changed with each other on the couch, the notepads from the colored folders were pulled out to the light and hidden again in their particular order. Anna felt better, as Sam thought she would. Her condition became more steady and the doctor had completely forgotten about the existence of

Anri Sammerson. But Sam received an unexpected phone call.

The professor was brief. He only asked if it would be convenient for Sam to come for a meeting the next Saturday, in the morning, before breakfast, and he provided the exact address. Sam could only say yes and ask for the exact time.

"7 a.m., Dr. Haley. We are having breakfast at 7 a.m. Please don't be late. See you."

The professor hung up.

Sam pushed the papers he had been working on, took the note with the address, and input the address into his phone navigation. The smart map showed him the route and determined the travel time as three hours and 36 minutes. He saved the address in the navigation app and was ready to leave the office, but another phone call caught him. It was somebody from the university saying something about a reunion. Sam didn't understand when, where, and why he needed to go; once again, he had been seized with a feeling that he was not in his right place and wasn't doing the right things. His heart pounded, and he felt a ringing in his ears and a lump in his throat. He sat down on the couch and leaned back, trying to relax and regain control of his thoughts and feelings. He succeeded, but not immediately. Sam had to sit staring at the smooth, plain ceiling for a couple of hours, until he finally realized that the heavy feeling had nothing to do with him. It rather was a premonition, but the doctor could not understand to whom it was related.

The week flew by and the next day he would be going on a trip to that extraordinary place. He, accidentally or not, found out some details about the clinic he was going to from the local police officer. The clinic specialized in mental disorders of women, particularly mothers who in some way had harmed the health of their children or even had tried to kill them.

Sam was sure that his trip would help him with Anna—it seemed to him that her case fit with the clinic's focus. He might even be able to persuade her to submit to inpatient treatment.

7

Anna left Dr. Haley's office and headed straight to her car. Usually there was no traffic on the road at that hour, and she never experienced trouble getting back home as well as to work on time. She lived on pretty strict schedule. Anna's workday started at seven a.m. every morning, then a regular eight hours plus an hour for lunch, and by four o'clock she was done for the day. After a quick stop at the flower store, she usually spent a couple hours at the cemetery.

She could not be counted among the fans of a long sleep, and it was easy for her to keep an early bird schedule. Anna had never been close to her coworkers. She did not have long conversations with anybody, just a couple of morning welcoming words and a late afternoon, "See you tomorrow." She asked questions related to work only. Nothing personal ever.

Anna's coworkers knew almost nothing about her. Their manager felt sorry for her and overlooked her oddities. He knew that Anna visited a doctor every Tuesday at lunchtime and always was late, but he never said a word to her, as if nothing ever happened.

Only one of Anna's colleagues showed that he was interested in her at the beginning. But as it turned out, he showed similar interest in all female colleagues, and with a few of them, he even managed to have a fleeting affair. But as soon as the women recognized him as a simple hunter for carnal pleasures, they lost interest and, as a rule, the "injured" ladies were transferred to other departments or even quit, once again smashing the hope for a speedy acquisition of an engagement ring. The "jeune premier" quickly realized that he would not archive anything with Anna, leaving off any further attempts, and finally he threw his keen interest to someone else. Anna never had lunch in the office, preferring to go a little far from the office's next door cafés, avoiding her colleagues. The only thing that she allowed herself at the workplace was tea. Anna loved to drink hot black tea. Many colleagues looked at her as if she did something wrong when Anna made herself a mug of hot tea in the middle of the 80-degree summer, drinking it with pleasure, not waiting until it cooled down.

Anna always drank hot tea using her own mug, the one she brought in her bag every day. Nothing special, a simple ceramic, dark blue mug with silver-colored views of a city Anna had never been in and most likely could not find on a map. Anna was not even able to read the name of the city written on the mug in Russian: "VORONEZH." Even if she could read the name of this faraway city, it would hardly have told her a lot.

That was the mug her mother brought from her native country when she was 17 and she treasured it all her life. It was a memorable gift from the man her mother loved more than anybody else: her grandfather. He remained in the city depicted on the mug, and of course, he had died long ago. Anna had relatives in that faraway country but had never tried to find them, the same way they never tried to find her.

Anna's mother, Maria, entered the country under the educational exchange program, but did not want to go back when her stay expired. She decided to stay in the country illegally, hoping to resolve the situation later somehow, and she could not even think about returning home. Her family had never forgiven her, only her grandfather, a wise old beloved grandfather from her father's side had always set her apart from the other 12 grandchildren, and she loved him very much. But unfortunately, after she had decided to stay, Anna's mother had no more opportunities to communicate with her grandfather. He was too old to oppose the will of his family, which had crossed Maria out from their lives and tried to forget she ever existed.

Maria had not graduated from school. A couple of months after arrival, she found out she was pregnant. She managed to get a job, rented a small apartment in a poor area, and continued to survive and believe that it would all turn out for the best. Even the challenge of living in a tiny apartment all alone, working 12 hours a day for little money, did not make her want to return to her native city.

Anna didn't know any of her family except her mother; it had always been a kind of a secret for her. For her questions about her grandparents, her mother always answered they were busy but would come soon and help them out and life would become better. Maria had always said this confidently, giving hope to Anna. But no one had ever come, although Maria hoped sincerely. Once she even went to the airport to meet her mother, but no one had appeared. For no reason, she had decided that her mother was going to visit the relatives, even though she knew that the whole family did not want to know anything about her anymore.

No one believed Maria that the father of her child was the disastrous fiancé chosen by her mother. And her mother had finally deserted her, not wanting even to talk to her on the phone.

Maria leaving the faraway country and never coming back had become a full-scale crash to her family who lived in a small country town next to the city on the dark blue mug. They had been planning her future, and per their plans, Maria had to pay back everything she "owed" to her parents. It was their opinion she had to pay back in a specific way: She had to marry the son of a local grocery store owner. The family had often taken food on credit and nobody had kept an accurate account of the debt because everybody was certain their most beautiful and intelligent daughter would soon become the wife of the spoiled son of the store's owner. Who would count the relatives' debts?

This promise warmed Maria's entire family, giving them the opportunity to survive the hard times of the '90s—times that were hard for the whole country where there was almost no food available in stores. The power had shifted; the government had changed. The enterprises, plants, and businesses had gone into bankruptcy, one after another. The workplaces had melted away. People lost their jobs, and their poor savings turned to dust. Even to buy a loaf of bread, people had to stand hours in a long line and then fight their hungry neighbors.

Everybody survived the best they could. People who were used to a specific system and all the things the system had been giving them for years unexpectedly found themselves out of the picture. There was nothing to build and no resources to use, and no one was interested in creating new ones. Government officials hadn't yet divided up what had been stolen, and less lucky people were busy digging in the ruins of their own lives, the next morning finding themselves with hangovers and hiding the rest of their pride back in dark closets until better times. The usual virtues had been devalued, bringing chaos to the souls of the recently minted free society.

They had dreamed of freedom for so long, and once they had achieved the material side of freedom, they filled themselves up to the top without leaving a chance to reach the true one. They had only changed one cage to another, with a bit more attractive appearance. Failing to obey the previous "diagnosis," they were happy to drown in another equally hopeless and absurd.

Only a few managed to escape, and the majority had followed the new gods, as usual not being too much bothered with the details. The air smelled of cheap perfume mixed with tobacco and different sorts of cheap alcohol. Many had chosen to drown in this sweetness, finding the boundless happiness of imaginary freedom.

Maria's father had not been an exception; he also liked to drink "the bitter" and had been fired during the first wave because of the addiction and could not manage to find even a crappy job. Her mother had never worked at all, as her "holy" duty had been to take care of their 12 children.

Maria was the seventh child out of 12, all kids a year apart from each other; the oldest was 22 at that time. Maria's mother told her there was nothing more important in life than to take care of her family, especially since not everyone got a chance like she did. The fact that she didn't love him meant nothing, as people said: "marry first and love will follow," and he was not the worst person and wouldn't hurt her too much. Anyway, she should be patient for the sake of her family. Maria hated with all her being the man who had been nominated as her future husband, and he in turn had seen in her nothing but a slave and another sacrifice. He had been known for perverse atrocities and had been caught a few times abusing pets. He had recognized Maria as his main pet who would tolerate his attitude because she had nowhere to go, and all her family's welfare would depend on the way she behaved.

When Maria had received an invitation to study abroad under the exchange program, as the student with the best test results, she began to hope for a better future. It took her tons of tears and promises to obtain permission for the trip from her parents. She had promised to come back and get married as had been agreed, assuring them that, with a foreign education, she could be considered a more valuable bride. The whole family suffered doubts during the following week, trying to decide on Maria's trip, and finally they concluded that she had no chance to escape and she would come back for sure.

Maria knew she would never come back. Her grandfather knew it as well because he had been entrusted with all her innermost secrets. He understood her, sometimes better than she did herself. He hadn't revealed her secret, even though he knew what that meant to the family. He loved her, and he had let her go. She treasured the memory of him deep in her heart, and he warmed her tired soul during the coldest nights.

8

Saturday morning was marked by a thunderstorm. A huge, black cloud moved on the peacefully sleeping city from the west, covering it with a wall of rain. It was still dark when the doctor left town, taking with him a few sandwiches and a thermos of coffee. The road took him to the north, to the mountainous area of the neighboring state. He had to drive almost four hours. In order not to lose time in vain, he took the recordings of sessions with Anna, from the first one to the last. Usually, the doctor did not record sessions, but he found Anna's case difficult and didn't want to lose any detail so that he could return to the nuances again and again.

He'd got his mp3 player connected to the car sound system and turned it on, right after he left the city and the traffic lights were not bothering him anymore. The speakers rustled. He heard slow, dithering steps, the person stopped halfway. Another step, also slow, but confident. Then his own voice came out of the speakers.

"Good afternoon, Anna. I am glad to see you. Thank you for coming. May we just talk? Please have a seat here."

"Hello. I … I don't know… I want… Mama… I am… I…"

"Do you like this figurine? You can take it. If it is hard for you to speak to me, try to speak to this figurine. Tell her what happened, and it will listen to you carefully. It will just listen, nothing more, only listen."

"I am tired… I am guilty… This is all me… Mom… I am… I… baby…."

"Do you have a baby? A boy or a girl? How old?"

"I am… I… child… yes… I… baby."

"Anna, could you please look right here. How do you think, is this cube real, one-piece, what do you think?"

A long pause, then a rustling and the sound of a slamming door.

Dr. Haley remembered his first session with Anna. He tried to run one of the simplest tests for schizophrenia, but after the question about the cube, Anna shook her head, stood up as if she remembered something important, and quickly left, loudly slamming the door. It seemed to him that she would not be back in a week, as they agreed, but he was wrong. Anna appeared at the appointed time. He switched the recording forward, skipping a few sessions in a row.

Again, sound of steps, a little more confident, but still not enough, another step, the same as on the previous recording, slow and confident.

"Anna, imagine that you found a time machine and you only have one trip, where would you go?"

"I would never…." A long pause. "Avoid the day of birth."

Anna's voice on this record was different from the first one. Her speech was less discursive; she more clearly expressed her thoughts, but still was lost in them and fell silent, not bringing the idea to a conclusion and then suddenly beginning to talk about something understandable only to her.

It was like playing with the radio when you turn up the sound, pulling phrases from the middle of the story, then turning the sound lower, not hearing the rest of the phrase to the end.

"Let's try a different way. What is the most memorable time you would like to change or forget? Maybe from your childhood?"

"Childhood… Baby… I want to change… I will change… We love to go to the park…"

"Tell me about it, Anna. What do you like to do in the park?"

"Ice cream, playground…" A pause. "No, I don't like people."

The last words sounded as if she was answering the question.

"Are you going there with your child? How old is your baby?"

I am… I… child… fun…" She was silent probably for 30 seconds, then the voice became anxious with shallow breathing. "Hurts." She paused again and her breath returned to normal.

"Yes, I love ice cream."

Sam switched the recording forward again.

"You look nice today, Anna. Is there any special reason?"

"I am just... It's my birthday."

The doctor listened to the recording, remembering that day, the first time she came wearing a dress. It was summer. Instead of her regular oversized warm jacket, she was wearing a light, bright dress.

Sam drew his attention to her beautiful body. Her loose hair was flowing on her long, thin neck, and her fringe was lying on the right side, playfully hiding her eyes when she lowered her head and tilted it slightly to the left.

"Oh, happy birthday! Are you planning to go out tonight? What do you usually do on your birthday?"

"We are going to the park and eat ice cream, a lot of ice cream, and then we are going home and turn on music and dance until we get tired. We will have fun."

"Are you waiting for the guests?"

"Guests? I... Mommy... I am... Baby..."

Anna's voice changed. Sam remembered that after these words, Anna's face had changed as well. Before that she looked unusually light-hearted, even happy, but her sickness came back. The smile disappeared, and her gaze turned back to nowhere. She pulled her neck into her shoulders and stooped, not allowing herself to be free and beautiful, as if she was expecting a blow from somewhere above.

The doctor pulled out a sandwich. He listened to the recordings, and it seemed to him that he had turned the wrong way at some point. Something did not add up; he had missed some important detail and was confused. Anna's words constantly contradicted each

71

other and sometimes she was confusing events. Sometimes she talked about herself in the third person, or perhaps she wasn't talking about herself. Sam didn't understand.

The road was winding, and the time flew insensibly. He was less than an hour away from his destination. He turned off the highway and 20 minutes later stopped at small gas station. He had a long day ahead and had run out of cigarettes. Sam got out of the car, pulled his credit card out of his wallet, but then realized that the gas station was so old there was no credit card system at the pump, and he needed to go inside to pay the cashier.

"Good morning! How is your trip going? How did you sleep last night? Do you need any help with your car? I know cars pretty good. I can even fix some minor damage."

The gas station guy was too friendly. His toothless, smiling face did not look healthy. But in general, he looked inoffensive. He was about 50 years old. His hands shook slightly, and his sparse, long, sleek hair grew below his neck to a sloppy tail but combed at the top to hide a bald spot. His nose supported huge, heavy horn-rimmed glasses with thick lenses. But in general, the gas station guy looked quite happy.

"Hi, I am good. Thank you! How are you? Please, a bottle of water and Marlboro Ultra Lights."

"That's it?"

"Yes, please."

"Here you go. $7.19 please."

"Thank you."

The doctor took his purchases and went to the door.

"You are a doctor, am I right?" The gas station guy unashamedly stared at Sam. "Are you going to stay with us forever or just visiting?"

"Excuse me?" The doctor did not get a chance to ask a question.

"I mean, are you going to live here? I am just curios if I need to open a credit account for your name or not," continued the gas station guy as if nothing had happened, pulling out from under the counter a huge notebook.

"Here, you mean, where?"

"Here, I mean, at home."

"I am sorry. I don't clearly understand what you mean."

"You are going to the Five Stars," which was the name of the clinic, "aren't you, Dr.? Of course, you are going to the Five Stars. What else would be out this way?" The gas station guy squinted at the doctor and bared his gums in a toothless smile.

The doctor stopped at the door, intending to open it, but changed his mind and turned around.

"Yeah, I am going to meet the professor."

"Well, all right, you can tell me your name later. I'll write you down as 'doctor' for now."

The gas station guy opened his heavy notebook and began to write the letters carefully.

"Have a good one, 'bye."

The doctor rushed to leave.

"Have a blessed day, Dr."

The gas station guy interrupted his work for a second and turned his attention to say his farewell to the doctor, gifting him with his unique smile.

The road meandered, taking the traveler higher up into the mountains and farther from the nearest town. The doctor had smoked several cigarettes in a row. After another couple of turns, he drove up to a tall iron gate. Sam got out of the car, leaving the engine running, and rang the bell, which was a bright red button right in the middle of the left door. The gate opened. Sam looked around, got back in his car and proceeded to the only way, forward. The road was narrow: Even two small cars would never be able to pass each other at one time. Each side of the road was lined by trees and thick bushes. There was no chance to swerve, no way to change your mind and turn back. *One way to the one end*, the doctor thought, feeling uneasy.

People said different things about this place. Residents of the surrounding farms, located in the low country, preferred to stay away. Some said there was military research taking place and experiments on human beings; others said it was a hospital for the most dangerous mentally sick criminals. Nobody cared what really was going on behind the high fence and steel gates high in the mountains, away from strangers' eyes.

The rare visitors preferred not to discuss anything, hiding behind the tinted glass in their cars, and the delivery of food and medicines had never been allowed closer than to the gates. All goods were reloaded into the cars belonging to the clinic and disappeared behind the gates along with the uncommunicative clinic staff.

9

"Dress up!" The mother was not happy: Her daughter was still not ready, dressed in old rags, hair not made, and still sitting with her useless books, the third hour in a row.

"Malik is not going to wait forever, show some respect!" her mother yelled and kicked the chair. The girl dropped the book from her hands, bent down to pick it up, but her mother had already kicked it far under the table.

"This is not important now!"

"I have an important test tomorrow, Mom. Is it so necessary to go out today?" Maria tried to keep calm, uttered each word carefully with caution, expecting a storm of her mother's anger, and she didn't have to wait long.

Her mother grabbed the girl's hand and pulled upwards, forcing Maria to get up from her chair, and as soon as she got up, her mother pushed her on the bed and hung over her like a dark cloud of imminent disaster.

"Don't you know what a hard time we are all going through? What should I feed you all tomorrow? You don't give a shit! You thankless bitch! Raised you for nothing! Your stupid tests won't feed the family!"

The mother was inexorable in her anger.

"I don't want to! I hate him and everything related to him! I would prefer starving! Please, Mom, please, I don't want to. He is sick; he hurts me all the time."

Maria was ready to burst into tears, but held them back, the tears of bitterness and not consent, but her mother didn't see, or rather didn't want to see. She had defined Maria as a sacrifice for the benefit of the rest of the family and was deaf to her entreaties and protests.

"Stop bullshitting! Everybody knows their family and respects them. They are kind to us. If his father hadn't helped us, we would have nothing to eat. You know how he helps us, so quickly get dressed up and get the hell out!"

"Mom, please." Tears appeared in Marie's eyes. She stacked the books with her trembling hands and went to get dressed. Marie thought that Malik would kill her eventually; she was afraid of him, but more, she was afraid of her own mother.

"And don't snivel in front of him! He's your future husband. It's okay if he'll get a taste a bit earlier." Her mother smiled acidly. "Look what we've got for dinner today." She put the bag with groceries on the table. "We all love you. Your pretty face works perfectly. We would be in trouble otherwise. So, don't be silly. Go on a date with your intended." The whole family moved into the kitchen. "We'll leave you a piece." Her mom laughed, picked up the heavy bag of groceries and went to the kitchen to make dinner for their big family.

Maria put on a simple dress, made her hair into a tight bun, wiped the tears, and went to meet her tormentor. She tried hard to calm herself, repeating like a prayer under her breath, "It's not for long. All a matter of time. Just a few hours and it's over. I just have to be patient. Time won't stop. Nothing is everlasting, and it all will end."

Her breasts were pressed by a heavy feeling of not accepting her own life. The heart refused to obey the persuasion of the mind, feelings and emotions raged against reality, but Maria could do nothing except obey the will of her mother.

The mother of the family was an unscrupulous woman, living only for herself. She had always led a dissolute life and not all of the children had been born in wedlock, but her husband didn't care. He was used to obeying his domineering wife. Maria's father threw up his hands and lived in his own reality, drawn into a hangover delirium. He didn't care about his wife's cheating, and the kids he considered nothing more than inevitable side effects of the well-fed family life. Her mother subconsciously had divided her children into those who were born from the "big love" after cheating, and those who were born from her hated husband, who according to her, had spoiled her life. She loved the children made through "big love" much more: She took better care of them and had never been rude or angry to them.

Maria was the unluckiest child, as she looked exactly like her father, and this fact put her in the worst place in the family. She had become her mother's enemy since her first breath. Marie was doing her best, trying to please her mother, but she only heard back that she was useless, stupid, and ugly, and for a while, Maria couldn't understand the reasons for such an attitude. Maria could only grit her teeth, endure, and look for any possible ways to escape from her mother's oppression.

Malik, Maria's intended, was the son of a local grocery store owner and was waiting for her outside the apartment. He was dressed in the manner and fashion of the times and looked weird. The pants were oversized, and the gold chain, worn over the sport jacket, looked ridiculous.

He spat chewing tobacco, hawked, and showed his dentures in an ugly smile; then he pulled Maria closer to himself, holding her with his greasy hands. She barely survived the kiss. The stench from his mouth caused a vomiting reflex.

"Well, well, my dear fiancé. Let's go," Malik said. His voice, his look, his smell, every detail of his appearance caused uncontrollable disgust. His continuous, uncontrollable burping accompanied him every single minute of his life. Malik stopped noticing his disease, but it was hard to be around him. He had disgusted everybody except his father, who raised him alone and spoiled him constantly. His mother left the sick child in the care of her despotic husband, who did his best to teach his son to hate women and everything related to them.

"I know you don't give a shit, but I have an important test tomorrow." Maria tried to avoid looking at him. A direct gaze always made him aggressive; she knew it firsthand.

"Hurry up. Let's leave for the performance."

"Aren't you happy to see me?" Black pieces of tobacco were stuck between his teeth and made his smile even more ugly.

"Ha, ha, come on, I'll show you a new stuffed pet. I bet you'll love it." He ran a hand over his bald, oily head.

Malik sniffed. His nose was strewn with dirty black spots of clogged pores. He pulled Maria's hand and dragged her toward his cave located in one of the garages across the road, ignoring the black holes of deep puddles left everywhere after yesterday's rain. Malik didn't notice anything around him and continued to drag Maria. Finally, she shouted at him and forced him to stop.

"What else?!" Malik hissed to her.

"I lost my shoe." Maria tried to defend herself. "I need to go back; it fell in a puddle." She pointed to the black spot in the middle of the roadway.

"Okay. Go, quickly," Malik muttered and let go of her hand.

Maria slowly walked back, thinking about why she didn't escape right then. Just run away, right now! Just run, run anywhere away from here, away from Mother, away from Malik, who wouldn't ever leave her and eventually would finally kill her and find another victim to play with.

She had heard she was not his first fiancé. He had another girlfriend, before they moved to this town, and she had disappeared; no one knew what had happened to her. Malik's father cut any gossip out at the root, threatened to close credit lines in his stores for anyone who talked about it. Maria never tried to talk about it to her mother, as she knew her answer ahead of time. Maria felt overwhelming, hopeless despair. She reached the ill-fated puddle, stuck her hand into the dirty water, got her shoe, shook off the water, and put it back on her foot. The cars were passing by at high speed, but Maria didn't care. She moved slowly, didn't look around, catching herself thinking that she would be happy if any of these cars hit her fatally, and it all would be over.

But that was not her fate, not her time; she knew it. She had a feeling that it would not happen that day, that way, and she just had to be patient. She had to go through everything, no matter if she was willing or not. She went back to Malik, looked at him askance; he grabbed her hand and, not paying attention to anything, dragged her forward.

The rusty door of his father's garage creaked. Malik pushed it with force and the door swung open. Malik pushed Maria forward and said,   "Go, turn on the light."

Despite all his made-up strength, Malik was a coward. He was even afraid of the dark, taking out his fears on those who were not able to stand up for themselves. Maria obediently walked into the darkness and breathed in the stench of a corpse of another poor pet. She felt the switch of a pendant lamp and turned the light on. Malik's cave was a sort of workshop where he was torturing and killing homeless pets, and then he mutilated their corpses, trying to make a stuffed animal from another victim.

The walls of the garage were hung with a lot of wooden shelves with ugly stuffed animals and a lot of glass cans with cut heads and guts of animals conserved in alcohol, mainly dogs, cats, and squirrels. Maria wasn't scared of them anymore. She tried not to look around.

"Look at this cutie." Malik switched on table lamp and turned the light to the stuffed animal: a black cat, standing in the middle of the desk.

Maria looked up at the stuffed animal and froze. It was a favorite pet of their subdivision, a cat named Kuzya. It wasn't possible to mistake his crooked leg.

Everybody loved Kuzya: He was an old, experienced cat, sweet and grateful. Neighbors let him into their homes, fed him, and allowed their children to play with him; he never scratched one child. The poor animal appeared in front of Maria in a horrific form.

The body of the cat was stitched hastily, carelessly, his belly smeared with dried blood; instead of eyes, he had holes in empty sockets and a scary grin on his face with a gray mustache.

It wasn't Kuzya's face anymore.

Maria could not hold back, and tears rolled down her cheeks. Malik had succeeded. Finally, he managed to make her cry. Neither the physical pain nor the humiliation could make her cry—she suffered in silence, and this fact infuriated Malik. But Kuzya was the last drop in the overflowing cup of her patience.

Malik brought the stuffed animal up to Maria's face. "Isn't it beautiful?" Malik was grinning with joy; he found special pleasure seeing the tears of the strong—until that moment—Maria. He made sounds similar to the howling of a coyote; Malik felt like a winner. He continued with pleasure. "First I tightened the rope on his neck, then I poked out his eyes; he was still alive, tried to escape, but I was strong enough." Malik was enjoying Maria's tears, as if he was eating honey. "It will be my wedding gift." He laughed morbidly. Maria broke free and ran away toward her home. Then suddenly she stopped, sat on the side of the road, put her face in her hands and sobbed aloud. No one was waiting for her at home; moreover, if her mother realized that Maria ran away from Malik, she wouldn't let her go for her test, and Maria would lose the only opportunity to escape.

She barely got herself together, got up, and slowly went back. Malik was waiting for her at the same place; he had no doubts about her return.

"Well, let's get back to our date." He put another batch of smelly tobacco, mixed with finely chopped dried marijuana leaves, under his tongue, took Maria's hand, and then led her to his home.

His father was never at home until midnight; Malik could do whatever he wanted. Maria was resigned to her fate and started to think about the time again. She whispered under her breath,   "Time does not stand still. I just have to go through it, just to go through it, once again."

10

Sam drove a few minutes until he reached a grassy plateau. With the opened view, it was impossible to guess you were high in the mountains.

In the middle of the neatly-mown lawn, to the left of the entrance, there was a beautiful house with four columns, built in a Renaissance style. The house was surrounded by a narrow paved path. A high, green fence spread along both sides of the house. Nobody was around, not surprisingly, since it was still early Saturday morning.

The parking lot next to the main entrance of the building had space for only a few cars. Sam chose a spot closer to the entrance, got out of his car, and before he closed the door, he saw a man appear on the threshold of the house. The man was not tall, of medium build, wearing a beautiful dressing gown over his shirt and trousers. The man stood on the porch and waited patiently while the doctor climbed the steps.

"Good morning, I am—" Sam started to speak.

"Right on time for the breakfast. Good morning, Dr. Haley, I am glad you came on time," said the man in the dressing gown, his voice calm and quiet.

"Professor?" The doctor asked dubiously.

"Don't be shy. We are all just at home. Come on, coffee should be ready."

"Thank you, Professor. I am so glad to meet you. I have heard a lot about you and your clinic—" the doctor said quickly, but the professor interrupted.

"No reason for cunning, Doctor. I doubt you have heard a lot about the clinic, but it doesn't matter. We will have enough time to say amenities to each other. Come on, coffee's getting cold."

The professor took the doctor's hand and led him away.

Professor Anri Sammerson was around 70 years old. He looked well cared for, natty, with soft facial features and a nice, low voice. His light blue, and now almost discolored, eyes created an impression of transparency, and at the same time, it seemed his eyes were wet as if tears were languishing on the threshold, not daring to appear. He wore glasses in a thin, almost invisible frame. Behind the gleaming glasses, his eyes created an impression that he was seeing right through you, and your most lurking, most private secrets, hidden in the depths of your soul and probably even forgotten by you, were opening by themselves.

But despite all that, Anri made a pleasant impression. His good manners were those of a gentleman educated in the traditions of an old school of the early 20th century.

They entered the house. In the small hallway, to the right from the entrance, was an umbrella holder with three umbrellas: one black, quite large, one dark purple, and the third one, bright red. On the left in the corner, there was a heavy coat rack made of wrought iron with nothing on it. Opposite the front door, there was a steep wooden staircase covered with red carpet, fixed on each step with a thin iron tube colored in gold with round knobs on the ends. The professor nodded to the door that was opened from the right side and kindly let the doctor go in first. They entered the dining room. It was not a large room, with extended floor-to-ceiling windows and drawn aside heavy curtains made of dark red brocade with golden tassels on the holders.

To the right of the entrance there was a fireplace that had never been used for its intended purpose—it served as a cozy shelf of the professor's memories. Just a few pictures in neat frames, arranged in a semicircle, as if a little company of friends had met to talk about the bygone days, and behind them, just at the back, there were two small porcelain urns. Opposite the entrance corner, there was a small semicircular buffet with glass doors and shelves. There were dainty vintage German crystal sets placed on the glass shelves.

A big, round oak table with sloping, gracefully curled legs stood in the middle of the room. On that day, Sam did not have a chance to look at the photographs or to see the crystal closer, although he felt a strange energy coming from this area, which was promising to tell a story which apparently was not funny.

"Please, have a seat, Dr. Haley." The professor pointed to the chair closer to the window. "Do you prefer plain black or with some milk added?"

"Just black, please."

The doctor sat down on the soft, comfy chair, made in the same style as all the furniture in the room. The chair was made from the same oak wood, had the same lovely curls at the ends of the legs, and was covered with a material that exactly fit the color of the curtains.

"Sure. Melinda," the professor said a little louder. "Would you be so kind to bring us a coffee pot?"

A moment later, the kitchen door opened, and a woman's head appeared for a second and then quickly disappeared.

"It's all right, Melinda. This is my guest, Dr. Haley. I told you about him the other day. From now on, he will come more often. He is not going to hurt you, I swear. It's all right."

The kitchen door slowly opened, and an older woman with partially silver hair, made up in a strict manner, came in. She was skinny, even bony, dressed in a long dark skirt, a white cotton blouse buttoned up to the last button, and a light blue apron with carefully washed out oily spots. Suspiciously glancing at the doctor, she put the tray with a coffee pot on the table and began to pour the coffee into cups.

The woman had a huge ugly scar surrounding her neck. It looked as if her head was sewed to her body with a few rows of rough stitches.

"Thank you, Melinda." The professor gently touched her hand. "You see, my dear, the doctor is the same as I am."

"There is no one the same as you are," Melinda muttered. She put the coffee pot on the table, gently freed her hand, took the tray, and hurried out of the dining room.

"Oh," the professor sighed. "Still can't bring peace back to her. I left off attempting. She is scared of almost everybody, except me, and that's why she lives in this house. I tried to move her with the other 'guests' to the separate house, but none of the attempts has been successful. As soon as she moves to another place, she regresses, her condition becomes worse, and it throws us far back. And we start the therapy from the beginning again—not from the beginning, of course, but pretty far behind her current, more or less fine, condition. Then after a few months, she starts to feel better, and she starts helping me with the household again. And by the way, no one ever asked her to do that. She decided once that she would take care of me and that's it. Whatever, I don't mind. She helps a lot. Don't be shy, Dr., we have a long day ahead; we need to eat and get some energy."

The voice of the professor sounded absolutely calm, as if nothing were happening.

"What had happened to her?" the doctor asked. "I have never seen such a horrible scar."

"Uh, oh, uh." The professor took off his glasses and wiped the lenses with a handkerchief, taking it from the pocket of his dressing gown. "This poor, little thing wore a collar made of razor wire, probably from the day she was born. God only knows how she avoided getting

86

an infection, dying in infancy or early childhood. I found her in a nearby, almost deserted village, when I was running around looking for a suitable place for my clinic. She lay on the floor next to her dead mother, whose body was already worm-ridden, and she was clutching her hand with her little bony fingers. Starving, poor child, she was hardly breathing. Her neck, or rather what it had become over the years of torture, had several layers of razor wire on it, and the wire was connected to a chain whose other end was connected to the same razor wire, but that one was on the neck of her dead mother."

The professor took a few sips from his cup and continued. "I don't know what happened there and why. I only know that the two of them were locked in the basement and someone was 'carefully' feeding them through a small window grate. There in the basement, I found traces that told me they were living in their cave for quite a long time. Most likely that's where she was born and grew up." The professor took a freshly baked croissant and spread it with butter. "She was, I guess, eight years old when I found her. Poor baby. I have seen a lot in my life, Doctor, but this scene shocked me." Anri looked up at the doctor.

Sam sat with all his attention riveted on the professor.

"Apparently, whoever locked them there had stopped bringing food and they were doomed to starvation. Her mother was giving her the last food they had and was slowly fading." The professor took off his glasses again, but this time to wipe his eyes. "The same fate was waiting for Melinda, if I hadn't found her in time. When I took her out of the basement and into the sun, the only thing she said was *angel*—she called me an angel. Perhaps her mother had told her about the angels waiting for them in heaven to help her not be afraid to die. Melinda thought that I took her to the heaven." He bit a piece of bread and quickly swallowed it almost without chewing. "I sincerely hope that whoever did this to them will burn in hell until the end of the universe."

The professor stopped speaking for a minute. His face reflected helpless resentment. He sent another piece of bread into his mouth and started to chew it diligently, venting the storm of emotions that swept him. Then he asked, "How do you like the coffee? Melinda brews delicious coffee, doesn't she?"

"Oh, yes. Yes, it is delicious." The doctor finally woke up and took a sip. "And croissants. I could kill for them."

The professor smiled. He agreed 100 percent with Sam.

Melinda was a skillful cook, despite the fact that no one had ever taught her. She begged the professor to bring her cookbooks and she spent many days conjuring in the kitchen, trying to surprise Anri with culinary delights. The art of cooking came to her easily; she had a natural talent and a special flair. She had never been even in the most rundown restaurant ever in her life, but nonetheless, she skillfully combined different ingredients and always creatively designed each of her masterpieces.

The professor always sincerely admired her talents, and Melinda took each of his kind words, however fleeting, as a happiness. Melinda took any critique quite calmly, carefully listening to the professor's comments, never feeling aggrieved. *You can't be aggrieved at an angel,* Melinda thought with a smile, listening to the professor's rare critique of her creations.

Anri and Sam continued their breakfast, discussing the weather and current market trends. Every time she entered the room, Melinda stood at the doctor's side. Her gaze was like the look of a puppy adopted by a wolf pack. Sam tried not to look at her, but curiosity prevailed time after time, and he stared at her scar secretly while Melinda was busy taking care of the professor. After they finished breakfast, the professor invited Sam to the terrace to smoke a cigarette. They came out of dining room back to the hall and turned to the right, passing by the stairs on the left, and entered the living room.

The living room was decorated in the best traditions of the Old World. The furniture was more than a century old, but well cared for and neat, as if just from the antique auction. The floor of the living room was covered with a huge Persian carpet, at some places faded, a bit shabby, but still impressive. The walls were a gentle cream beige color. Two small chairs with a marble table between them found a place left of the entrance. The backs of the chairs were made with a kind of hill going down from the outside to the inside, forcing people who sat on them to be close to each other.

A beautiful crystal vase with fruit stood on the table, and a small porcelain saucer with a thin sharp knife sat right next to it.

The wall behind the seats was decorated with a well-made copy of Eyck's *The Virgin of Chancellor*

Rolin. Tiepolo's *The Immaculate Conception* hung between the chairs, while above a marble fireplace there was Veronese's *St. Helena: Vision of the Cross* and at the right side Lotto's *Allegory of Virtue and Vice*. On the mantelpiece right in the center, a porcelain, well-dressed horseman jealously guarded St. Helena "sleeping" above his head, and on both sides of him, a few porcelain couples entertained him with their minuets: ladies in their best outfits with cute cavaliers and a lonely horseman, in love with the ephemeral Helena.

On the opposite wall, there were six long mirrors in carved frames painted the color of the walls, creating the impression of weightlessness and between them were five gilded candlesticks, each with three slightly melted candles. A cozy couch with a wavy back and a pair of the same intricate soft armchairs were pushed back from the mirrored walls, close to the middle of the room. A low coffee table, covered with a handmade starched lace cloth, stood right in the center between the couch and the chairs. Huge windows opposite the entrance served as the main room lighting. Light curtains were drawn apart; the sun had risen long ago and was already warming the soft fibers of the carpet. Every single thing in the bright warm room was filled with warmth and love; it seemed to Sam he could even breathe easier.

They walked across the room and went out to the terrace through the door hidden behind the curtain to the left of the window. Sam took out a cigarette and started to touch his pockets, looking for a lighter, then he remembered he had left it in the car. Anri noticed his confusion and offered him a lighted match.

"Thank you." Sam lit his cigarette.

"I still prefer the old-fashioned way, matches. When they burn out, they leave a smell of sulfur in the air. You may find it funny, Doctor, but I like that smell. It reminds me of old times."

"Nothing weird—honestly, you're not the only one who likes that smell. As a child, I loved to burn matches, just for fun. Auntie scolded me for that, but to no avail. I continued my experiments until I burned her favorite curtains in the kitchen. She didn't cuss, but was so upset that I decided to leave that dangerous game. Now I use the fire only when indulging the stupid habit of smoking."

"I totally agree. It's a stupid habit, but I can't quit. I started smoking immediately after I opened the clinic. I can't allow myself to drink, if only for extremely rare exceptions, you know; many 'guests' have bad associations with the smell of alcohol, but no one cares about a tobacco smell. So, I can smoke, although it's a doubtful pleasure. Have you ever tried to quit?"

The professor lit a cigarette and coughed.

"I never thought about it, at least not yet. By the way, thank you for meeting me during your private time on the weekend, Professor. I'm flattered."

"Private time? My friend, what are you talking about?" The professor smiled and gave Sam a meaningful look. "We don't have private time and weekends. The thing we are doing here is not work; this is our way of life. Our life itself. My life, for sure. This is my home. By the way, thank you for coming, Dr. Haley."

Sam noticed the strange gaze of the professor. There was something ambiguous in his smile, something that brought that weird, uneasy feeling back, that uncomfortable feeling, which didn't allow Sam any rest for the last few days, causing his heart to jump out of his chest, his breathing to quicken, and his mind to race.

"Oh no. I'm so glad I am here." Sam smiled. "You know, I'm working on research related to the mental injuries of children, and I thought you might shed light on some questions I've been stuck with and give me your advice or even show me some of your most vivid cases—of course, if you deem me worthy enough."

"Hmm. The most vivid cases." Anri frowned slightly. "Tell me, your research, is it for publication or for you personally? I mean, I want to understand if you are trying to make a name and to improve your business or you just want to help people?" The professor coughed.

The question did not confuse Sam; he was expecting it. "This is not the right theme for making a name. Too inconsistent and too many *buts* and *ifs* occur in each case. Everything is so individual and so special."

"Hmm, you are right," Anri agreed, satisfied with Sam's answer.

The doctor hesitated for a few seconds and continued. "I met one woman, a girl—I mean, patient—at the beginning of the year." Sam paused, then continued a little awkwardly.

The professor never had a habit of interrupting and waited patiently while the doctor was picking up the right words.

"I can't understand her. I mean, I can't get if she is telling truth or if all the things she speaks about only exist in her imagination." The doctor's voice became more emotional. "Initially, I diagnosed postpartum depression, but after a few weeks, it became clear that I was wrong. I missed something. I think there is continuous sluggish schizophrenia as well, but I can't stop having doubts, and I feel it is not an easy case. I am worried about her. So I really need your help, your experience, if you don't mind, Professor."

"You're saying sluggish schizophrenia, hmm, you are worried. Well, that's good that you are worried. It's interesting." The professor frowned and faintly smiled. "And how does this case connect to my specialization?"

"Oh, I forgot to mention that she has a child. At least, it seems so to me," the doctor said apologetically. "But she never gave either the baby's name or gender. Moreover, according to some things that she talks about, it can be concluded that she may cause physical harm to her child, and of course, mental harm could take place as well."

"And what does my friend Officer Richards say—you know him, don't you? Does he know her?"

"I don't think he knows her. No, for sure, he doesn't. I met her accidentally, or rather, she came to my office, but did not dare come in. I was late that day and I met her at the door in the elevator hall. My intuition told me that she needed help and I offered her the sessions, but she replied that she didn't want to be treated. I asked her if we could just have a talk. So we started our weekly sessions. But I'm not really her doctor, and she's not really my patient. I asked her for the sessions, citing my research. I know she needs medical help, but I can't push her, can't assign regular treatments, and of course, cannot force her, and persuasion won't work, I'm sure. It's difficult to talk to her at all, and it seems to me that her case requires a separate approach, but I can't define it. I was hoping, frankly, for your help, Professor." Sam said all this quickly, almost in one breath, then raised a questioning gaze to the professor.

"We would have to talk in more detail about it." Anri ground out his cigarette and immediately took another one. "However, anyway, I would have to meet the patient in person. We will come back to this a little later, if you don't mind." He held the burning match to the cigarette pressed between his fingers and it began to smolder.

The next few minutes they stood in silence. The professor was deep in thought, and the doctor did not dare to break the stillness. The sun was warm outside. The morning breeze shared its freshness with the two brooding men standing on the terrace. The professor was smoking and coughing badly, while Sam enjoyed the beautiful mountain view.

Anri had made a decision already. He finally realized it now. He had no more doubts: Sam was the one he was looking for. Officer Richards had checked Sam's background, and Anri liked what he found out. He only had to meet Dr. Haley personally to finally verify the accuracy of the choice.

But time was short, he should try to hand over to him as much as possible.

"Okay, enough for us smoking and relaxing," the professor said, a bit excited, and threw out his third cigarette in a row. "You didn't come here for smoking, right? Let's go—I'll show you everything."

Anri and Sam went back to the dining room, passing the living room filled with sunshine. Coffee was still waiting for them on the table; they drank the leftovers, and even though it had already gone cold, the coffee still was delicious. Melinda had the professor's jacket ready and waiting for him on the coat rack in the entrance hall. Anri changed his outfit and they left the house. They went down the outside stairs, passed through a narrow alley surrounding the house on the left, and reached a golf cart parked on the side. The sky was cloudless. It was hard to believe that there was a storm four hours out to the south.

"Please, Doctor, don't be shy." The professor pointed to the golf cart. "Take a seat, please. This is my indispensable means of transportation. Our territory is not that small, not easy to walk around, especially for such an old guy as I am." Anri coughed. "Better to save energy for other things, trust me."

Both took their places in the golf cart and rode through the path around the house. A wider road lay in front of them after they passed the green fence. The doctor was surprised at what he saw. At both sides of the road, Sam saw houses, just regular houses, built in a row, running for a few miles. This fact would not fit with others in Sam's mind. He opened his mouth a bit, looking around and trying to see local inhabitants.

Each and every house looked so tidy and well cared for. He noticed green backyards with lots of flowers behind some of the houses. It looked more like a small fairy town under the warmth of the mountain sun, protected from all sides by giant cliffs. The "town" was still sleeping. Lazy dogs were barking in some of the backyards.

To say that Sam was surprised was to say nothing. He couldn't speak a word. The professor looked at his astonished face and smiled sarcastically. "Did you expect to see gray, faceless buildings with grates on the windows? I can guess." The professor turned the golf cart to a narrow dirt track. "Isn't it beautiful here?" He stopped next to a three-story house.

The doctor looked around and said, "It can't be named a mental hospital, Professor, at least, not in its traditional appearance."

They stepped out of the golf cart, passed by the low hedge fence, and found themselves in the yard. A fat Siamese cat was napping on the bench under the lilac tree; he looked spoiled with attention and treats. The cat opened one eye, looked at both visitors, and turned away to the backrest of the bench, not finding them even a little interesting, continuing to ignore the vanities of the world silently.

"I told you, we are not working here; we are living here." The professor knocked and the door creaked.

"Good morning, gentlemen." A pretty, older woman stood on the threshold and smiled pleasantly at the early guests. Her dark hair was tucked under a kerchief of pale blue, tied beautifully on her head. She was dressed modestly. She was wearing a white silk shirt with a lace collar, with all the pearl buttons buttoned, and a dark blue, straight, midi-length skirt with a sleek pearl-color belt with the same pearl buttons. Here heel-less shoes were made of soft leather in a nude color. She was tall and moved gracefully with an obvious dignity.

"Would you like to have breakfast?" She motioned them into the living room.

"Oh, no, no, Isabelle, thank you. We had breakfast already." The professor proceeded to the living room, stopped by the cabinet at the right wall between two open kitchen doors, and opened the upper door of the cabinet.

"Please, come in, Doctor." Isabel kindly welcomed the doctor, as if they were already introduced to each other.

"Okay, what do we have 'hot' for today?" Professor took out of the cabinet a thick registration book and sat on the couch, putting his feet on the ottoman.

"Please, have a seat, Doctor. Oh, my bad! I forgot to introduce you. This is Isabelle, our head nurse."

Isabelle nodded to the doctor.

"This is, Dr. Haley; I told you about him a few days ago," Anri explained to Isabelle.

"I got it," she answered.

"Okay. Let's see, nothing serious." The professor was looking through the notes in the book. "Isabelle, did you contact Officer Richardson today?"

"Not yet, Professor."

"Please give him a call and find out when he is going to bring Ms. Tears with her little Andreas. And,

97

please, don't forget to arrange everything necessary before they come. Three stars. For sure, three. Three for now, then we will see."

"Sure, Professor. Don't worry. I'll get everything done."

Isabelle took a new empty folder and drew with a red ink pen three little stars on the upper left corner.

"Thank you, Isabelle." Anri put the opened registration book on the coffee table next to the couch. "Well. Dr. Haley, we are waiting for your questions, if you have any." He raised his head and stared at Sam with a prying gaze.

"Hmm." The doctor did not find what to say right away. "I have a lot of questions, Professor." He smiled. "I think you know better what to start with."

"Ha, ha, sure, Doctor." Anri smiled fatherly. "I have a lot to show you and much to teach. We are short on time."

Anri continued to smile, as fathers smile when they hand over a family business to their grateful sons. Sam was surprised by the professor's gaze, but he did not attach much importance to it. At the end, it wasn't the strangest thing he had faced that morning.

"Okay, Doctor, this is our registration book." Anri pointed to the table where he put the book a minute ago. "Here we write down the most important things that must be done during the day and after that make notes and comments, depending on how things are going. Also, we make notes on some, for the first look, small, negligible actions, and signs." The professor was speaking slowly. "For example, yesterday, Isabelle drew attention to the fact that the door of the neighboring house no longer pops so loudly as before, a small thing that tells us, who know what is going on, a lot. For me, a smoothly-closed door means that after seven years, Caroline has ceased to withdraw into herself and is ready to take the next step toward her ultimate recovery, and this means also that the method of treatment, which was applied to her unusual case, worked out exactly as we expected. So we're on the right path, Doctor. It's important to know your way and follow it without turning, in spite of all doubts."

Professor turned the page. "Here's another small detail. Yesterday afternoon Adele found her ring that had been lost a few weeks ago. Of course, we always knew that the ring had never been lost. Let's say, it had been borrowed, and we know by whom and always knew it, and we also knew why and how to fix it. And this is our victory, a small one, insignificant on the scale of the universe, but so long-awaited, a hard-won victory over the disease of another unfortunate creature, with whom we make ant steps day by day, always moving toward the light."

The professor, his mouth parched, asked Isabelle for a glass of water. After a few sips, he continued. "We start a new book every calendar month. The necessary notes are added into the personal case of each 'resident,' let's call them so, Doctor, if you don't mind. Based on these notes, we can see a clear picture of the disease and life in our 'town.' We store all books, without exception, in our archive. I'll show it to you later and will give you one book to go, to look through when you get a chance."

Sam was about to respond with thanks, even though he didn't really understand how this book could help him, but the professor continued to speak without a chance for Sam to say a single word.

"Go through the book. If you have any questions, feel free to ask. I am telling you that we are short on time." He smiled in a fatherly way again. "Okay, let's go, Dr. Haley, and leave Isabelle to do her job." They stepped out of the house. "Let's smoke a cigarette and move forward."

The professor offered a lighted match to the doctor. The "town" slowly began to wake up. Voices could be heard and Sam tried to listen attentively. Regular talk, people wishing each other good morning, talking about the weather and pets, discussing new recipes and stories about children's antics. All quite common for a tiny town, except for the fact that this was a mental clinic, and everyone who lived there were, to a greater or lesser extent, sick.

"Nice woman, isn't she?" The professor pulled Sam back from his thoughts. "Her help is invaluable and she is irreplaceable." Anri started coughing; a minute later he continued. "She is one of those who we have been able to help. One of those who has completely recovered."

The professor got Sam's attention in full.

"Isabelle was around 10 years old when she came to the clinic along with her mother. She was born and raised in the big city and at first it was hard for her to accept the local rules and lifestyle, but eventually she got used to them. She allowed us to help her, and we did our best to move her talent and energy in the right direction and not give her a single chance to endanger herself with her youthful inexperience."

100

The professor ground out his cigarette; Sam had already finished smoking. They sat in the golf cart and drove down the road.

"And so, Isabelle," the professor continued. "She thought that she could cope with her sick mother, get her to feel better with her boundless love and self-denial, despite the fact that her mother's state was getting worse and they could not live a single day without another mental breakdown, after which she didn't remember anything. Every other breakdown brought Isabelle a new scar. Her mother was not able to control herself. Isabelle was hiding all these facts for a long time. She was afraid to be apart from her mother. At the end, the ambulance brought the girl to the hospital with a severe brain injury. She scrambled out and opened up about the truth to the officer. He brought them here."

They turned to another road, which was taking them out of "town," closer to the forest. "It took us a long time to get her mother's mind in a better state so that she was able to control herself. They both received the appropriate treatment. Isabelle needed help no less than her mother did. And after about a year of them living here, we finally were able to leave them alone for the whole day, without worrying about the consequences."

The road was taking them farther and farther from the main part of "town," hiding the roofs of the houses behind the trees. "After graduation from high school, Isabelle went to university and then to medical school; she chose to study psychiatry. After graduation from the medical school, she returned to us, but in a different role. Trust me, Doctor, I didn't ask her to come back; it was her choice. She didn't come alone; her husband joined us as well—you'll get a chance to meet him later. They met at the university; however, his specialization is general surgery. By the way, have I mentioned that we have our own little hospital?" Anri smiled proudly. "Isabelle is one of the few who knows our life from the inside, I mean, those few, who faced the disease and recovered. Her help is invaluable."

The professor stopped and lit a cigarette; he had started to smoke more in the last few months and was coughing harder each time.

Anri and Sam turned past the trees. The doctor opened the other side of the clinic, which was not as bright and carefree as the one they just left. Sam felt as if he had crossed the line between the light and dark side.

11

Heavy buildings made of brick with grates on the windows towered over the picturesque lawn with majestic mountains in the background. Nothing scary at all, but in comparison with the "light side," the difference was striking. It was quiet: no dogs barking, no trifling talk, only the rustling leaves of nearby trees and the timid whispers of the wind.

Five identical four-story buildings, with a sixth, or rather the first if you count from the road, that was two stories and the main building. They parked next to it. The professor lit a cigarette without leaving the golf cart.

"How often do you cry, Doctor?"

"Cry?" The doctor lit a cigarette too. "Not that often; I don't really remember when the last time was, but it happens, probably like everyone else. Sometimes emotions take precedence over the reason and restraint."

"Don't worry, Doctor, and forgive me my interest. The emotional side of people I find interesting. Emotion is our true face. Every mind falls under influence of emotions. Even those who consider themselves unemotional, cold-minded, and circumspect act under the influence of an emotional condition. They fall prey to emotions, which define their path, choosing the mask they wear for the rest of their days. Emotions and feelings drive actions, both the good and the terrible."

Sam was listening quietly.

"Each of our actions, whether we like it or not, makes us experience certain feelings and emotions; this flow of incessant emotions we used to call one short word: mood. In actual fact, our mood is the emotion, experienced during a certain period of time and united in one single thing. And the mood itself, as you know, is an inconstant thing."

The professor raised his head and looked at the sky. A thundercloud, which followed the doctor from the city, finally caught up and appeared close, promising a big storm.

"Let's go, Doctor." Anri opened the door and they entered the hall of the main building. High ceilings and wide, dark hallway with several doors and stairs to the second floor were at the end of the corridor. The reception desk was right next to the stairs. The thick smell of medicines hit the sensitive nose of the doctor;

it seemed that the walls themselves smelled of medications.

"Good morning, Lola." The professor spoke quietly, but with noticeable alarm. "No incidents?"

"Good morning, Professor."

A beautiful, young brunette lady sat at the desk and smiled pleasantly. She had dark, almost black, hair made up in a neat style, decorated with three studs with pink stones, faintly gleaming, refracting the bulb light. She was dressed in a dark blue shirt with two small pockets on both sides of the chest, tucked into straight black pants with a high waist. Sam couldn't help but notice her perfectly-shaped body.

Her every motion was full of impeccable severity and dignity. The unfathomable depth and mystery of her bright green eyes, edged with a thick line of black eyelashes, left Sam speechless. She was like a goddess of the night, descended from heaven, and by some error got stuck on the Earth after the dawn.

Lola looked at Sam with some interest; she slightly nodded to him and smiled. Sam thought he felt himself filled with soft warmth, covering every cell of his body, disarming him and engaging in a conspiracy with mysterious, magical powers.

"No incidents," Lola said, without taking her eyes away from Sam.

"Good. You have newcomers today. Ms. Tears we discussed last week."

"Sure, Professor, I remember."

Her voice was soothing. Tuneful, low, without any drop. This voice could declare a war, and it would be taken for good news.

"Great." The professor took a bunch of keys from the top desk drawer. "And we also are going to move Inna to town today. I think she is ready. Would you mind bringing her case to my office, please. And we would be happy to have some coffee, as well. Thank you, my angel."

"Of course." Lola smiled and graced Sam with warmth of her gaze again. He got a bit confused and unconsciously took few steps back, as if he was a shy student who met the prom queen in the school hallway.

"Oh, my bad again! I am so sorry, my dear, let me introduce you to Dr. Haley. I told you about him."

"Nice to meet you, Dr. Haley." Her smile turned Sam speechless again. "Welcome!"

"Nice to meet you. Thank you," Sam barely uttered.

They went to the second floor and left Lola to her routine.

The professor's office did not look like a demanding place. It was nothing special: a small room, desk with a bunch of different papers around a laptop, old office chair, and a pair of brown leather armchairs with low backs for visitors. The windows were dusty; no one entered the professor's office without him, and he was too busy to devote his time to cleaning.

"We are here for a few minutes, Doctor, but, anyway, please take a seat." Anri sat on his chair and turned on his laptop. "Sorry for the mess. Can't find time to clean all this out. Frankly speaking, I do not spend here a lot of my time. I prefer to work, as we say, 'in the field.'"

"Oh, it's okay, I understand fully. I still haven't gone through the boxes I brought to my office from my practice; it's been five years and they still are gathering dust," Sam said and sat down on one of the chairs.

"Today is an important day for us, my friend. We are moving one of our patients to the town." The professor stared at the monitor for few seconds and continued. "She is almost recovered and is able to live a normal life, of course, under our strict supervision. At least for now. And then, who knows, maybe she will want to return to the "big world."

"So, you discharge sometimes?" For some reason, the doctor was surprised.

"We are not discharging, Doctor, we are letting them go," the professor said meaningfully. "It's hard to believe, but no one is forced to be here. Everyone came to us on goodwill, one way or the other. Someone asked for help, someone had been highly recommended to accept our help. But I repeat, everybody here made this decision themselves."

The doctor had already ceased to be surprised. He just listened carefully, taking note of everything the professor was telling him.

"Most of them have been forwarded to our clinic by my good friend, a police officer. We've worked with him for many years, became friends when he was investigating one case long ago. He also has good friends in different states, and those, respectively, also have some connections and so on." Anri pulled from a bunch of papers one piece and gave it to Sam. "This is his direct contact. I know you met him once, and you'll get a chance to know him better, he is bringing our new guests today."

"Guests or patients?"

"Patients—I don't like this word, Doctor. It dehumanizes and makes us look at the person as a folder with a history of the disease, rather than the history of his life, where the most important key to recovery is hidden. For me, they are all guests. We take them, trying our best to do everything in our power, and then let them go if they are ready, and most important, if they want to go."

The professor coughed, cleared his throat, and took a sip of water from the half-empty bottle he took from under the table

"Not everyone who comes to us for help can be defined as a patient." Someone knocked on the door. "Come in, please."

Lola brought a coffee pot and a couple of cups. The doctor was confused again, but this time, he tried not to show it. In his nighttime fantasy, the woman of his dreams looked exactly like Lola. He was waiting for her clear and warm-as-a-spring smile, but Lola was worried about something. She went up to the professor and whispered something in his ear. Anri thought for a moment and just as quietly answered in her ear. She frowned and quickly left the room.

"Professor, can I ask you? Lola, she, pardon my curiosity, was she also sick?" The doctor paused and tried to hide his eyes from professor, fearing exposure of his secret nocturnal fantasies.

"Oh. No, no. She is one of those good souls who just helps us. Again, on their own will, but certainly not entirely free. I will tell you everything, but these things are simply something you should be aware of." The professor poured coffee for both. "Let's get some quick cheer and start our morning tour."

Lola was still sitting at her desk when they went down the stairs. The professor returned the keys to the top drawer, made some notes in a regular working manner, and they went outside.

"Keep up, Doctor."

They entered the second building.

There was a small reception area, more like a concierge room, with a three-tiered stand with pots against the far wall. The top pots had blooming begonia and the lower two had rich cissus. The stand looked like a green waterfall with white foam on the upper edge. Sam stared at the green "waterfall" and did not notice Ray, the "owner" of this little miracle and actually the person in charge of this building.

A young man, tall, thin, with thick blond hair, attractive and neatly dressed in a shirt with mixed colored squares of gentle pink, blue, and light purple, and light blue straight jeans. He smiled broadly and greeted the professor. Sam had been introduced to him the same way as the others, without further ado.

After a short conversation about current issues, Ray handed Anri a tablet, similar to any other tablet, with only one difference: it had a card scanning slot at the upper edge. The professor picked up the tablet, motioned Ray to follow them, and they all headed for the stairs, climbing to the top floor. The corridor with light walls ended with large window with grates covered with morning glory blossoms. A long, rectangular pot stood in the middle of the windowsill. It was painted in the same color as the wall and windowsill, and therefore had been nearly invisible at first glance. The window looked more like a three-dimensional, glowing picture.

On both sides of the corridor, there were three doors made of solid wood with glass inserts in the middle. They went to the farthest door. On the wall to the right of the door, above the line of sight but with easy arm access, there was a small, almost invisible, plastic pocket with a plastic card in it.

The professor scanned the card found in the pocket at the door and received access to the personal case of the patient staying in the room. Anri quickly read the last line and, satisfied, returned the card to its place.

"Good job, Ray!" Anri said to the man who was waiting for the outcome with noticeable worry. The man smiled and went back to his working space.

The professor knocked and after a few seconds opened the door, and they entered. Sam was surprised that the door wasn't locked. The room looked just like any other room; the only difference was the grating on the window.

"Good morning, Sophie. You look nice today!"

A young girl dressed in a home suit and slippers sat at the dressing table in the right corner of the room, brushing her wavy hair. She smiled and greeted the professor.

"Today is a beautiful day, isn't it?" She made a fluffy ponytail, got up, went to the professor, and hugged him. "I slept the whole night through! He's gone. He is not hurting me anymore." She glowed with joy. "After I spoke to him yesterday, he is really gone."

"There we go! I told you he would give up! I congratulate you on your victory!" The professor was genuinely happy and did not hide it. They looked more like friends than like patient and physician. "What are your plans for today?"

"I was thinking of reading some books about child care, and I am going to learn swaddling and the right way of holding when feeding. Time is short. And I need to learn a lot."

"Great plans! You're clever!" Anri kissed Sophie on the forehead. "I'll stop by tomorrow and you'll tell me about successes in swaddling. And please do not forget to take the medicine; we should complete the course and then will try to go without it." The professor spoke softly and slowly. "Okay, we have to go, see you soon."

They left the room and the professor gently closed the door. "Later, my friend. I'll tell you later."

They visited all the rooms on the fourth and third floors. Hope lived behind each door. All the women were young, no older than 35, but each one had gone through personal tragedy already—the most terrible tragedy, the loss of a child—but not all of them were aware of it.

On the second floor, there were common rooms—dining room, kitchen, living room—and a couple of rooms with entertainment, books, board games, and various handicraft. The ground floor was given over to medical and household needs.

After checking the state of each "guest," Anri and Sam went outside, leaving Ray with his daily duties. Anri offered to sit down on the bench next to the nearby lawn and smoke. Sam did not mind.

"This is the building of 'the Lost.'" The professor took a deep breath, held it for a few seconds and let it out, nodding slightly, as if giving himself permission to continue. "That's what we call them. Each of them for some reason has lost her child. Some of them even don't know about it; it all depends on circumstances of each single case." Anri spoke slowly, clearly pronouncing each word and then looked at the doctor. His look was the same as the look of a child who tells his mother about a new friend as if asking her opinion about him.

"Sophie, the young woman we visited first, she doesn't know that her baby is dead." The professor's gaze had changed. "She has been with us for half a year, but her mind returned to her just two weeks ago. She doesn't remember those six months. They do not exist for her. It's good. She only remembers the last two weeks."

"I don't quite understand, Professor, what do you mean? How is that possible, that they don't know?"

"No one ever told them." Anri changed his voice to a teacher's tone. "And no one will! They will remain happy mothers who give their love to the children who are missing it."

"That means they will raise somebody else's children, without even knowing about it. Isn't that legal?"

The doctor was still undecided about how he felt. He actually felt little but deep confusion.

"Somebody else's? No, no, for them, they are their own. It doesn't matter," Anri paused. "Sometimes lies help to save. In this case, two lives. At least two."

"I don't understand. How do they not know?"

Anri turned his eyes to the tree next to the bench, pursed his lips slightly, paused for a moment, but soon nodded to himself again and said, "Sophie was

111

brought to us on the brink between life and death, almost immediately after she delivered a baby. Her husband, a rare piece of scum, had been poisoning her and the baby in her womb with potent drugs. He was driving her to madness, playing out crazy scenes and assuring her that nothing had happened and that she was imagining things. She believed him. And he was feeding them with poison. We barely saved her life. Her baby didn't make it."

It seemed to Sam that the professor's eyes became wet. "What kind of monster would kill his wife and not allow his own child to be born, for the sake of money? I refuse to understand it! I don't want to! I'm afraid even to imagine that any kind of excuse could be found for such a heinous act. For me, there could be no excuses." The professor lit a cigarette. Smoke hid the wet gleam of his eyes. He took off his glasses, wiped them, and then wiped his wet eyes, pretending that nothing had happened. He put his glasses on again and said, "She didn't even see her child. Sophie regained consciousness here in our clinic. It took her half a year to return to normal life. For her, these six months flew by as just one day; for us, as another life. Every guest is the life we must live through and we are living through together; otherwise we won't be able to help.

The professor turned away as if he saw something, wiped his wet eyes, and continued. "We are taking newborns and children up to a year old, abandoned by their parents. We give both a chance for a happy life. A little daughter is waiting for Sophie. She gave birth to a girl six months ago. In a few weeks, we'll move her to the town along with the baby; they will live in a house with a nurse who will keep an eye on both. If all goes well, Sophie and her daughter will return to the big world after some time. They both will have a second chance for happiness. Is that so bad, Doctor?"

"I don't know." Sam was confused. "Maybe you are right. How did it happen that she is here?"

"Her parents, fortunately, returned from an international trip earlier than planned. Her mother felt sick and they came back home. They immediately figured out what was going on and called the ambulance and the police. Then the officer recommended they bring her here. It's all simple."

Anri stopped speaking. Sam wasn't going to break the pause; he took out another cigarette, but remembered that he had no lighter and was going to put it back into the pack, but the professor noticed and handed him the matchbox.

"Take it, Doctor. I have another one with me. I always have a few, just in case I forget one or drop it somewhere." Anri coughed and took a cigarette for himself.

They both were hidden behind cigarette smoke. Sam needed a break, and the professor was tormented by doubts. He wasn't sure if Sam would understand and accept the principles and practices that had been painstakingly created here. The methods had been designed and improved by many successes and failures, responses and reflexes; everything had been carefully protected for years for the benefit of those who found shelter behind the thick stone fence of the clinic—those who had already returned to the "big world" and those who were going to return later.

He suddenly doubted in the correctness of his choice. Despite all Sam's characteristics, Anri still feared that he was not ready to take on his shoulders the burden of responsibility for the life of the guests—past, present, and future. In the end, they all were woven into a subtle weave; all were connected to each other.

It was one thing to help, as we do when we give alms or donate money to different foundations. It seems if you helped someone, you're a good person, that you saved someone—or maybe ruined someone? Help is not always necessary at a certain place and is not always good. Sometimes even the sincerest minor help may completely destroy someone or at least bring about the beginning of the end.

The professor had a rich experience and knew that not everyone always needed to be helped. In some cases, the best way to help was to leave the person alone with difficulties and give him a chance to resolve them and to grow. But the line was so thin: Would Sam be able to recognize it and stop on time? Anri had so little time to teach him. He would have to rely on Sam's natural gift, and he had no doubt of its presence. But any talent needs training and development. Did Sam have enough strength and patience, as Anri had during all these years?

The questions choked the professor, but no one could give him an answer. Time, only time—he needed to give him time and try his best to be around as long as possible. There were so many questions, so many answers waiting in the wings. Anri closed his eyes, nodded to himself. Anyway, he had no choice; he wouldn't be able to take care of the clinic soon, and he needed a successor.

"These five buildings," Anri nodded to the brick houses, "we call them the 'Five Stars.'" Anri raised his eyes and looked at Sam. The doctor met his gaze with the clear understanding that his life was going to be changed forever soon. The professor liked the signs he could read in Sam's eyes; he nodded to himself again and continued to speak. "When we are waiting for a new guest, it's enough to say how many stars, and the staff then has some understanding of the reasons and can be ready for further procedures.

"One Star is the building with abandoned children, newborns up to a year. We have older kids, but only as rare exceptions. Two Stars is the building of the Lost. We visited it today. Three Stars is the building with women who have severe postnatal depression transformed into much more serious mental disorders, who never have been treated accordingly, but their condition is still reversible. Four Stars is the building with children who suffered at the hands of their own mothers who are staying in buildings Two, Three, and Five. But even their children have the right to know their mothers. Have the right to forgive them. Have the right to love them."

"How many stars today"

"Three Stars. Ms. Tears and her baby. She asked for help herself, after she threw her child out of the window in another fit of anger in the middle of the night."

"Oh, Lord."

"The boy was lucky. He fell on the canopy right behind the window and didn't suffer physically at all. He just got scared. We'll put him with Madison's family. They have been living in our town for a long time. And they'll take care of him as if he is their own, but we'll also let the mother see her child. We won't hide him. A couple of weeks under our intensive treatment with our methods and Ms. Tears will be able to see her baby. Then, if all goes well, we'll put them together in the town—of course, under supervision. Well, then, who knows? Maybe they'll go back to the 'big world.' Most likely."

"Most likely," the doctor repeated quietly.

"Our guests are coming and going away, leaving us with invaluable experience and emotions."

"Are you okay, Professor?"

Anri suddenly turned pale and swayed a bit.

"Yes, yes, I am fine, thank you! It's all right, my friend. Let's go. It's time for lunch."

"Wouldn't we," Sam stammered, "won't you visit the other patients?"

"Later, Doctor. I think you've gotten enough impressions for today."

They climbed into the golf cart and drove back to the town. Meanwhile, the thundercloud was getting closer and closer, covering the tops of the trees with dark shadows, trees that sheltered flocks of local birds from the upcoming storm. The wind gusts became stronger and stronger, raising the dried, recently mowed grass from the lawn, carrying it across the county as gospel. Rain dripped, and the smell of the trampled dust and impending thunderstorms came right in time. The violent downpour as emotion, flashes as bewilderment, and thunder as final consent.

12

Every Sunday in "town" began with going out for breakfast. It was a kind of tradition, helping the "guests" to better get to know each other and share experiences of getting out of difficult life situations, and from the other side, it was an excellent opportunity for the staff to notice insignificant changes. All the families agreed in advance who would go where every other time. The professor visited one of the families every Sunday. During the year, he managed to visit every house personally. Anri trusted his carefully selected staff, but still preferred to monitor the state of patients who moved to the town, feeling his responsibility for every life entrusted to him.

Sam had to stay for the night; the storm had raged since early evening and left no chance to return home safe, and besides, he saw no reason to take a risk, as no one was waiting for him at home. He was happy to spend another day with the professor, to get to know him better, to learn the local rules and conditions. They talked until two o'clock in the morning. The doctor had time to reflect on everything he had seen and heard during the day; he could not fall asleep for a couple of hours and finally gave up to drowsiness right before sunrise.

A gentle knock awakened Sam the next morning. At first, Sam couldn't figure out where he was since for the last few years he hadn't woken up anywhere except his own bedroom or office. He quickly got himself together.

"Just a minute, please." The doctor jumped out of bed and put on a dressing gown borrowed from the professor. "Please come in." His voice sounded sleepy.

"Good morning, Doctor." Melinda entered the room slowly, as if fearing something. She brought the doctor his clothes, carefully laundered and ironed. Sam thanked her and asked if she could leave him alone so he could dress.

"Oh, sure. Excuse me, Doctor." Melinda blushed, realizing the awkwardness of the situation. "The professor is waiting for you in the dining room. It's breakfast time." Melinda smiled and left the room, leaving doctor to himself.

Sam sat back in the bed and looked around the room. He hadn't had a chance to explore it last night. The bedroom was designed in the same style as all the rest of the rooms in the house, but it looked like this room belonged to a young woman. Pale pink walls, and a light wooden bed with carved headboard on the right from the door in a little recess. Nightstands were made of the same wood and stood on two sides of the bed, both covered with handmade patterned tablecloths. Lamps, made in the form of candles, were mounted on the headboard of the bed. On the left from the door there was a wide antique dresser painted in delicate, almost transparent colors of pink, light green, and peach. A few porcelain figurines depicting the daily rest of a shepherd surrounded by three pretty shepherdesses decorated the top of the dresser. On the opposite wall, next to the window, there was dressing table with an ottoman pushed under, and a large oval mirror in a wooden frame right above the table, all items from one set with the same delicate pattern on the edges. There

118

were wide windows covered with white tulle and gentle peach curtains.

The doctor got the feeling of someone's presence; it seemed to him that the woman who might once have lived in this room had just stepped out and would come back shortly. This feeling was so strong that Sam rushed to do all his morning activities, quickly put on his clothes, and stormed out of the room. He reached the stairs in two steps and came down to the dining room. Being worried by the strange feeling of a presence, he dressed so quickly he didn't even notice creases on his jeans, carefully ironed by Melinda. Jeans with creases looked weird with his casual shirt.

Anri, dressed in a holiday suit, was sitting at the table, reading the newspaper for last Friday, humming some song under his breath.

"Good morning, Professor."

"Doctor! Good morning! How did you sleep, my friend?" Anri greeted Sam without taking his eyes from the newspaper.

"Pretty good. Thank you, Professor." Sam finally found the time to look at the pictures languishing on the fireplace mantle.

The first picture was a wedding, a happy, just-married couple with their family. Happy faces letting the couple go to their new happy life, and a note on the bottom written with beautiful cursive: "Good Luck, Anri and Anjelika Sammerson, October 1962." The next pictures told the story of their traveling. Two persons who seemed almost as one, their faces similar, their eyes and hearts turned to each other, and the dates, carefully written: 1963 and 1964. The last picture stood on the right in a gilt frame, shabby in some places, thus giving it special value, making it proud of being often taken in hands, wiped, and hugged to the heart. The same young woman was in the picture, but without a man; she was holding her child, and she looked lost, like a soulless doll, her face drawn with indifference, without even a sign of tenderness in her eyes, so familiar to Sam, staring into to the distance, with a neat inscription at the bottom: "To dear husband and father, Lili is six months today. With love, Anjelika, 1968." The doctor stared at the photo as if he was waiting for it to explain to him what had happened.

Sam looked at the professor. He was still reading the newspaper, not paying any attention to him. Sam did not ask a single question, if the professor deemed it necessary, he would tell him; if not, let it remain his personal drama.

Anri laid his newspaper aside and finally turned his attention to Sam. "Excuse me. I can't understand some things that have taken place in the world. I feel sorry for the people. So how did you sleep, Doctor?"

"Very well. Thank you."

Sam noticed that the table was completely empty, contrary to his expectations. Sam was hungry and hoped for delicious coffee with fresh baked croissants, but there was nothing but the professor's newspapers on the table.

"I see Melinda took care of your clothes." Anri did not hide his jokey tone. "All my pants are done the same way. It's actually not that hard to get used to it."

"Professor, since I had to stay for the night, might we have another day of visiting? I mean, the buildings."

120

"Afterward, my friend, afterward. First, we'll have breakfast with a wonderful family, Molly and Kate, and after, we'll need to visit their curator, Bella. Didn't I tell you yesterday about our Sunday's breakfast tradition? Some people are going to church on Sundays, and we are going to have breakfast." Anri got up. "Let's go, my friend. I bet the breakfast is ready and waiting for us."

They came out and the professor lit a cigarette as he usually did. The golf cart took them to the house of Molly and Kate. One of many other houses in this town, particularly unremarkable, surrounded by smooth lawns with neat flowers in front of the porch. There was a white door with the number of the house and names of the guests who were living there. In the upper left corner, Sam noticed little stickers, three almost invisible stars that informed local staff of the main necessary details. Finally, the door opened, and on the threshold, they were met by a beautiful, young woman dressed in a holiday outfit with multicolored stripes, with a skirt that just covered her knees. Curled in neat ringlets, her long, blonde hair, fixed with a headband, slid over her shoulders.

The open door let the morning sunlight in, and it burst into the room, giving a warm glow to everything. The woman was glowing too. Sam forgot for a moment where he was. He thought that he was a little boy knocking at the neighbors' house, and the mother of the family, who was spending her happy life with her family in her own house, had opened the door. The smell of fresh baking with cinnamon, almost forgotten because of his aunt's allergies, took him away into his childhood to the days before his parents died. The voice of the professor brought him back to reality.

"Molly! You look great! Good morning!" Anri walked into the house first, hugged the woman, and introduced her to Sam. "Dr. Haley this is Molly. Molly this is Dr. Haley. And where is our wonderful Kate?"

The professor looked around. The edges of the tablecloths hung down to the floor, and Anri noticed a slight motion while a child's voice giggled, barely restraining itself. The professor pretended he hadn't notice anything and went straight to the table.

"Well, it's time for breakfast, and I'm starving. I'm sure you all are too, so let's eat all the most delicious food while Kate is not here." The professor spoke loudly and clearly, winking to the doctor and Molly.

"Oh, yes, Professor, you are right! Time to eat!" The doctor picked up on the game.

"All the most delicious food at first!" Molly also caught the game.

They all sat down on soft chairs and pretended they started breakfast. They heard rustling, and Kate finally popped up from under the table; one nimble leap and she was already crumpling the professor's lap.

"Aaaa, got you!"

"Kate!" The professor hugged the girl, then tickled her, and she filled the room with her ringing laugh. "You are right on time!"

She was a six-year-old girl, skinny, with blond, almost white, hair and big blue eyes with long, nearly invisible, eyelashes. She wore a bright blue dress with a knife-pleat skirt, and a butterfly made of bright red and green sequins shimmered on her chest. Kate looked happy and toothlessly smiled, sitting in the professor's lap. Her holiday dress was rumpled, and the bow in her hair had moved down to the back of her head, but she did not attach any importance to this. She had a piece of paper in her hands, and she finally decided to give it to the professor.

"Look, I drew it myself." Kate handed the paper to the professor. Her face was expectant with a slightly-parted mouth. Her eyes looked into the professor's, trying to predict his reaction.

The professor looked at the paper for a minute. Kate did not take her eyes off him, then Anri frowned slightly, Kate cocked up her ears, and finally the professor smiled.

"I've never seen a cow cuter than this one. Isn't it the one who gives chocolate milk?" At that moment, it was possible to feel physically all the warmth and kindness that the professor shared with everyone who was around him.

"Right!" Kate showed all her remaining teeth, smiling widely. "How did you know the milk is chocolate?"

"Well, people call me 'Professor' for a reason!" He laughed and put the girl on the floor; she hurried to take her place at the table.

They had breakfast and talked about different things. Molly was a great cook, and her cookies deserved special attention. Sam was looking at her and couldn't believe this pretty woman could once cause harm to her beautiful child. They both looked so perfectly close, so tender. Sam did not notice any hint of troubles. They looked like a happy family. The only thing that he noticed was the way Molly looked at the professor: Her eyes were full of boundless gratitude. She was thankful to the universe for giving her a second chance at happiness. She wouldn't fail this time; neither she nor the professor had any doubts. By the end of breakfast, Sam had a feeling he was visiting old friends; everything was so easy and clear, no tricks, no worries. Molly and Kate were so happy, sincerely enjoying the wonderful morning and company of their guests.

"Thank you, Molly, for the delicious breakfast! I'll see you next week. We will discuss all the details." Anri hugged Molly.

"Have a wonderful day, Anri. It was nice to meet you, Sam."

Molly followed them to the door. Kate hugged the professor and whispered something in his ear instead of saying goodbye. He smiled in response and nodded with a serious look. Anri and Sam came out of the house and both automatically lit their cigarettes.

"They both look healthy. They look like a happy family. My intuition keeps silent. I don't feel any tricks. I used to trust my feelings before."

"Don't you worry, my friend, your intuition is fine. As of today, they are a happy, healthy family, if we can say so." The professor coughed. "They are 'living' with us for two years. They've spent one year in town, and one year, the first one, in the buildings. Both completely recovered, thank God."

"I can't help but ask, you know." Sam looked at professor with guilty gaze of curious child.

"Of course! I can't help but tell you." Anri went to the golf cart, with the doctor in tow. "I will tell you on the way." They went toward the distant houses, located near the forest, occupied by the clinic staff.

"When officer brought the girls to us, Molly was already at the brink of nervous and physical exhaustion. Several breakdowns in a row, hard work. Kate was sick all the time, which was not surprising. Huge medical bills and aggressive bill collectors, never enough food, and in their house, it was either too hot or unbearably cold. Molly had several jobs trying to get out of trouble and make it better. This is the paradox of the system: daycare is not affordable, too expensive if you are paying all the bills yourself. It is not that easy to survive, even if you're making average money. Well, not the essence. Molly worked as a waitress in several places taking extra shifts, and it didn't leave her time for the child. She dreamed that something would change, maybe she'd meet someone or would find at least one friend she could rely on, at least mentally, emotionally. Molly tried not to allow a single weakness, never complained, never cried; she struggled, gritting her teeth, was suffering, hoping. But in the end, she finally lost control of the situation first, and then of herself."

They stopped at a one-story house. The professor lit another cigarette.

"Molly grew up in a shelter and could not allow her baby girl to have the same fate. She tried struggling. But it's always difficult to be alone. A human is still a gregarious animal. She wasn't strong enough. She broke down and was ready to commit the irreparable. Molly couldn't allow anything to deprive her of the child. She decided that it would be better if they both went to heaven; at least, they would be together. She gave up. Neighbors became concerned only when they smelled gas. They called 911. Both girls were rescued.

125

The officer brought them to us, took them from the hospital under his personal responsibility. They've been recovering here."

After all these years, it became harder for Anri to control his emotions; he always took every single case to heart. He let into his soul all the pain and all the fears of unfortunates and went a long way with them on their road to recovery. Shoulder to shoulder. When Anri was telling Sam about their patients, he remembered every detail of every problem, every little special thing of the particular disease. Every nuance that led them to the state they were not able to control. In these minute details, he sought and found the way to their recovery.

"Is it so hard to give a hand of support?" The professor's face expressed an extreme degree of desperate bewilderment. "I mean regular life. People could help each other, at least emotionally, not waiting until they are asked for help. We could be a little more attentive to those around us. Not everyone, my friend, can ask for help. Many people simply don't know how to do it. It's easier for them to die than to ask for help."

"Yeah, we would have much less work if people were a little more attentive to each other." Sam stared at the wheel of the golf cart, covered with dirt after the previous day's thunderstorm. He understood perfectly what the professor was talking about. "Most of my patients are quite successful people, by today's standards, but they all come in to talk. They lack attention, although they live in big city. At first glance, there shouldn't be a lack of communication. Another paradox of our time. Too many people, too many friends, but everybody suffers from loneliness and taking their places in an endless line to

126

psychotherapists' offices, just to talk. Just to get a piece of attention."

"In a perfect world, my friend, psychotherapists should not exist; there should be just friends and close people who are ready to listen, neighbors and those who care, those who are not drowning themselves."

"And we could have more time to devote to the real diseases, instead of rectifying the consequences of extreme selfishness." Sam tried to smile, but was unable to portray anything but a sad face with crooked lips.

"We'll have more than enough work for a long time."

"By the way, Professor, how familiar are you with the internet?" Not waiting for the answer, Sam continued. "I am astounded at the crazy willingness to help any stranger on the other end of the world whose photos are posted on social networks, while ignoring the ones who are around and also in need and not less deserving to be helped."

"Yes, yes." The professor smiled sadly. "Who do you think, Doctor, has more chances to eat tonight: a starving and ragged child whose photo was posted on social media, or a similar poor little thing who is asking for help on the street? It seems the same people are passing by him, the same humans who just an hour ago transferred their money to the account of another fund with plaintive photos. No, not all of them are fake, but many. And how much money out of those millions will end up with that hungry child?"

Both lit another cigarette. The doctor's cigarettes had been depleted the previous night and he had to borrow some from Anri. They were smoking for a while, silently, when the professor continued. "Why is it easier for us to help the myths? Why not to feed the child of your neighbors if you see him starving? Eventually, leave some money under their door, incognito, just as you do over the internet. Or give him some food, as if by chance. It's not a child's fault that parents can't take care of him. And it doesn't matter if they are trying their best or not. From the fact that you'll condemn his parents, saying they could work more or not have children, this kid won't get any better! Your reasoning and arguments won't warm him up, even if you are 100 times right. He doesn't care! He is hungry!" The professor coughed heavily. "Why not try to help someone next to you: perhaps you are his only hope for salvation from hunger, coldness, or just from loneliness, in the end. Maybe after talking to you today, he'll find the strength to change his life tomorrow and won't make mistakes; at the turning point, he will stand next to somebody else saving another life."

The professor stopped speaking. They finished smoking in silence. The morning sun had already cleared and began to heat the tops of the trees. Birds chirped, flying from tree to tree, sharing the details of yesterday's storm. Anri and Sam had a long, busy day ahead. They were short on time.

13

That Monday morning Gina came in earlier than usual. She entered the office humming some happy song and opened the window. Her face glowed with happiness. She was smiling to the new, happy day. The weather was clear, and the sun pleasantly warmed the world with its soft morning rays. There was a gentle breeze and the air smelled of fresh rolls from the bakery across the street. She usually tried to stay away from the bakery, but not today. Gina dialed the number of the bakery and ordered a dozen fresh croissants with different fillings. The coffeemaker hissed, signaling that the coffee was ready. Gina once again, probably the hundredth time that morning, looked at the ring on her finger. The huge diamond set in gold gleamed, as if winking at Gina, assuring her that she wasn't dreaming, but really was getting married soon.

She finally had met a person who was on the same page as she was concerning life and hopes for the future. It was okay that he was not the most handsome—it wasn't the most important thing. The most important was that he loved her, and they had a lot to talk about and sometimes to argue about. They both loved nature and wanted to live outside the big city, and the most important point for her was that he wanted to have a baby, and not just one, if they were lucky. And of course the feelings. She caught herself thinking that she might love him the way she never had loved anyone before. But she was scared to admit it before all these wonderful things happened. What if he wouldn't enter into her feelings, wouldn't want to be around her? Gina's mind tried to keep her heart safe, as it had been broken so many times and reassembled from a thousand pieces, but it remained clean and kind.

The Friday night dinner with Matthew's parents went perfectly. That's exactly what Gina dreamed of. The perfect way to meet his parents and to get engaged: fancy restaurant in the heart of the city, beautifully dressed people around, delicious food, relaxed atmosphere at the table and an unexpected offer of marriage at dessert, with a beautiful ring in a glass of champagne.

He kneeled on one knee, everything in the novels about "the big and pure love," asking her if she would like to make him happy and marry him. She couldn't hold back the tears, answering yes. He put the ring on her finger, and they hugged and both realized finally that they belonged to each other.

Gina liked Matthew's parents; they were nice people who had achieved everything by hard work. They brought up their son in the old traditions with respect for family values. Finally, their son had made a choice. They were ready for grandchildren and were looking forward to when their son would find his soulmate, not daring to impose their own will, allowing him to find the one with whom he would live his life in love and harmony. Matthew's family was fairly rich. They owned a farm in the south of the neighboring state. Matthew, in turn, had graduated from a university with a degree in veterinary surgery and was interning at one of the city hospitals. After interning, he intended to return to the family home to continue the family farming business along with his own veterinary practice in his hometown. Gina charmed him with her simplicity and directness, open-mindedness, and her trust in people. During the short period of their relationship, she managed to surround him with care and warmth, which he did not want to be apart from. Gina was attentive to his habits and preferences. For example, every morning Matthew loved to race to the hot shower, jumping out of bed when the alarm started to ring, and Gina was always up a few minutes earlier, turning on the water in advance so it had time to heat up and fill up the entire bathroom with steam.

That morning procedure amused her; it wasn't difficult for her to get up just two minutes earlier, and for Matthew, it made every morning with Gina especially joyful. He appreciated this seemingly small thing. Just two minutes earlier, and his day was made.

The delivery guy brought the croissants. The coffee was ready. Nothing could ruin the morning—that's what Gina thought, and she began to sample the freshly baked croissants. She had to tell the doctor about her leaving because of family circumstances. Family! The word swirled in Gina's head. She was going to have a family, a real family! Of course, the doctor would be upset, but he'd understand and let her go with all the best. She would invite him to her wedding. Gina had so many things to do ahead of time: finalize the list of guests and complete the wedding gift registration. Gina was so busy with her thoughts she did not notice how another croissant had disappeared into her mouth.

"Good morning, Gina." The doctor's voice sounded as if it was floating.

"Good morning, Dr. Haley," Gina answered. She hadn't noticed when he came in. "I'll need to talk to you, Doctor. Whenever you get a chance."

"Sure. What about after lunch? As soon as Anna leaves. Oh, Gina, I forgot to ask you. Please cancel Mrs. Fadden's session. And assign her time to Anna."

"Oh, Mrs. Fadden. Yes, sure, Dr. Haley," Gina said unconfidently.

"Yeah, I know," Sam smiled slightly and pursed his lips as if apologizing, "but what can I do. In the end, she's just a human and she's not going to hurt you. At least physically. Especially via the phone. And for God's sake, do not transfer her to me. Tell her I had to leave urgently for a family emergency, or drowned in the bathroom, or just died. Whatever."

Gina smiled.

"I owe you," Sam added, and went into his office.

Mrs. Fadden was the person who inspired fear and distaste in Gina. She looked like one of Gina's middle school teachers. The one who used to comment on Gina and a few others in a sarcastic manner, disgracing them in front of their classmates. Even without these comments, Gina had never been popular.

Every day the teacher chose one of her *favorite* students and practiced her standup talent with gibes addressed to the unfortunate. The poor child was subjected to humiliation in front of the whole class. She did not hesitate to ridicule the appearance as well as the quality of clothes that her victim was dressed in. She expressed her doubts about the mental development of the student. Parents of one of the unfortunates tried to complain. But she had been honored a few times, including Teacher of the Year, and the school administration only replied that it noted the complaints. And the teacher continued her experiments on the endurance of the children's mental health. It looked like she was taking out all her anger of her unhappy life on the poor children, all her hatred which she had saved up during many years.

Thank God all that was behind her. But Gina still had nightmares, as if she was standing in the middle of the classroom completely naked and the teacher threw out gibe after gibe, and all around the other children laughed, pointing at Gina, teasing her.

Mrs. Fade was not only similar in appearance—her personality was reminiscent of the nightmare teacher. On the one hand, Gina was afraid to dial her number and inform her of the cancellation, but on the other, she was glad she wouldn't see her scary face. In the end, she could tell her all the information fast and hang up. Or leave her a message, if she got lucky and Mrs. Fadden didn't pick up her phone. Gina dialed the number and held her breath.

"Hello." Gina heard the answer from the phone. "I am listening," said the squeaky voice with a hysterical tone.

"Good morning, Mrs. Fadden," Gina mumbled. "This is Gina from the Dr. Haley's office. I regret to inform you that doctor will be out today because of a family emergency. So we have to cancel and reassign your appointment, unfortunately. I will check with Dr. Haley on his return and call you back. Have a nice day."

"What? Hold on!" Mrs. Fadden interrupted. "What family emergency? I need to talk to him right now! Give me his cell number! Now! Otherwise I'll come down there and rip out the remnants of your disgusting withered hair!" Mrs. Fadden nearly screamed.

Mrs. Fadden was using the position of the psychotherapist patient pretending to have a mental disorder. She didn't hesitate in using certain expressions and insulting anyone who met her in the doctor's office. People thought of her as a sick person and didn't pay

133

attention. But Gina, due to her painful memories, feared her as a nightmare.

"Dear Mrs. Fadden." Gina gathered all her courage. "I'm not authorized to disclose any personal information, including cellphone numbers. And I am not going to give out the doctor's private cellphone number to you or to the pope himself! You got it, Mrs. Fadden?" Gina elevated her voice. "If you have any concerns for the doctor or for me personally, you are welcome to stop by and I'll put the remnants of my—as you said—'disgusting withered hair' into your filthy mouth, so you'd choke on it!" Gina took a deep breath

The voice on the phone went silent. Gina thought for a second that Mrs. Fadden would have a heart attack, and for a second, she felt guilty. But the voice came back to life.

"I-I-I…" Mrs. Fadden groaned. "I don't want to see you. Ever! And I-I will find another doctor. I'll file a complaint."

Short beeps. Gina took a deep breath and exhaled. Gina felt as if a huge stone had fallen from her neck. She has been keeping a grudge against her teacher, transferring it from year to year. She was projecting her fear onto other people. In everyone who had ever hurt her, she saw a piece of the person who had undermined her confidence in childhood. Finally, she was freed from the power of the childhood resentment and answered her offender using their own weapons. Her cheeks were burning; she felt heat and a strange delight.

"It's not as scary as it seemed," Gina said to herself. "She's just a human. With weaknesses and fears, and she must be an unhappy woman, if she behaves this way." Gina finally calmed herself.

Gina felt for Mrs. Fadden a kind of pity mixed with contempt. The coffee in her cup had gotten cold, and she got up to pour herself a fresh, hot drink, trying to decide which type of Dr. Haley's patients Mrs. Fadden belonged to.

The majority of the people who had been fraying their pants on couches in the doctor's office, as a rule could be specified by a few types.

The first type—bored ladies seeking rich men, some already wives and some who had not caught their luck yet and were still living as the "other" woman. They just wanted to talk about themselves, about how beautiful they were and how they were undervalued by their husbands, lovers, family, friends, or whomever else. Each of them was absolutely assured in her uniqueness, although they all looked nearly the same. The doctor could barely distinguish some of them because of their similar plastic surgeries.

Once Sam even had a session during which he was fully confident that he was talking to one person where in fact it turned out that it was another patient entirely. He was lucky the patient never noticed his confusion.

Just as with their appearance, their problems and concerns were also often identical. On that unfortunate day, the "plasticine lady," which is what Gina called them, had been concerned that she didn't have enough time for everything she needed to get done in a day. First, she had to get up and eat her specially-made, exclusive diet breakfast, apply her morning makeup, then work out at the gym, spending 10 minutes walking on the treadmill with her best friend on the phone. Then off to the swimming pool, after which she attended her regular appointment at the beauty salon. Then daytime makeup and time for daily shopping, as she needed to monitor the trends and buy the latest fashion and accessories to look appropriate.

"I don't even have time to stop by some cozy place for lunch, and all these traffic jams—oh, it's so horrible" was the sort of thing she usually complained to Sam about. And she needed to find extra time to apply her evening makeup and to choose the way she would look when meeting her husband, if he deigned to appear, and if he didn't appear, then she would go out to some fancy restaurant with her friends since there was "no reason to hide this beauty at home."

On that day, she almost had a mental breakdown. She pulled a mournful face and with a nagging voice told the doctor she had spent her morning running around and looking for a belt made by some fashion designer. She even missed her workout, and when she finally managed to find the city's only boutique that carried the designer's belt, one "shrew" had bought the last one! The last out of 212 belts produced for the whole world, and that shrew had grabbed it right in front of her nose, and then the patient had a nervous breakdown. Fortunately, since she needed a new color for her nails and hair, the breakdown hadn't lasted long and she was able to make her beauty salon appointment.

"I was saved." She was seriously concerned. "But what if next time I won't be able to help myself? I am scared to even think about it."

The doctor had been listening to all this crap coming out of the mouth of the spoiled courtesan, but he professionally endured, keeping a serious, concerned face. He had been saying some clever words while giving a name to her condition, and then prescribed vitamins and convinced a patient, hungry for peace of mind, that the prescription would help. He flatly refused to prescribe to such patients a serious medication. In his opinion, the stupidity of some of the patients was such that they could accidentally kill themselves by taking an overdose. The doctor did not want to take that risk, and furthermore, there was no need to prescribe anything at all. Unfortunately, no one had invented any medicine that could cure idiocy and stupidity.

Another type of client usually consisted of couples who had been lost in everyday household turmoil but still hoped to save their unhappy marriages. The doctor paid enough attention to them and tried to help find a way out of their situations if he could still see any. He knew that the primary diagnosis of the majority was boundless selfishness. But it's not easy to cure selfishness, especially if the "disease" had sprouted from childhood and had been lavishly fertilized by caring parents all during childhood. Such "forever suffering" couples usually consisted of males who were the users or scroungers and females who were the "princesses."

After several attempts to help such a couple, the doctor obtained a clear understanding of the hopelessness of any such efforts. He'd been indignant, expressing his opinion about such people to his best friend, Green Joe. Sometimes Sam addressed him with a long, emotional speech to blow off steam.

"Boys being raised as users." The doctor was boiling over. "Their mommies wiping their asses until high school. As a result, they grow up selfish, not even able to take care of themselves, and have the opinion that everybody owes them something. They need someone to take care of them, to cook, to wash, to clean, and even to earn for them, because they are freaking miracle creatures! And girls! They are raised like princesses, told from the beginning that it's enough just to be beautiful, just to be able to take a 'cool' selfie, pump up the ass and get bigger tits rather than growing naturally. It's okay! We can get implants! The main thing is that the mother's ambitions will come true. She will get a living Barbie doll, the most desired Barbie doll. Who cares that the doll is not able to feel real love, not able to care, not able to give birth since her body will be out of shape. And who the hell cares about her brain, erudition, interests—no one needs them. No one needs her opinion. Finally, the Barbie doll would not need the spoiled idiot with narcissism syndrome next to her because she needs someone to take care of her as well as believing that everybody owes her something."

Dr. Haley was yelling. Green Joe as usual agreed—what else he could do? The cactus seemed sometimes more soft-minded than Sam appeared to be when expressing his deep, hidden thoughts. "And the worst thing is that society indulges both in every way." The doctor for a long time sat thinking about the eternal questions.

The third type of patients were lonely people. Almost all of them suffered from unconscious mental injuries from childhood. Many of them could not even articulate their own desires or dreams. Some of them, conversely, were overconfident and surprised by the fact that they had not been noticed and appreciated accordingly. Sam tried to help both, often spending more time than planned. And again Dr. Haley brought his complaints to his best friend Green Joe.

"By killing our children, we are killing our future! It is not clear what they want to see tomorrow when those parents maim their children today. Suppressing their personalities, depriving them of interest in life, nipping in the bud any aspirations. It's so easy to destroy, but try to create, to direct, to get the child interested." Sam was pacing his office, looking at the cactus on his desk. "Traumatized children in time will grow up and become adults with mental diseases! Am I right, buddy?"

Green Joe agreed.

"What did you say? Yes! You are right! We are raising maniacs and perverts. Indulging them in everything from early childhood, trying to protect them, hiding, telling them that we know better about what, how, and where to go, but protecting them from what? From life? They eventually grow up as stupid slaves who have never made any decision, protected from all kinds of problems, all kinds of thinking, with candy in their mouths in order to keep them quiet and not bother us. And here you are right again! Then, when it comes time to say a word, make a decision and take control, it's not happening because the child can't even make an egg himself since he had never done it before. So, who is to blame for what is happening in society? And I do not feel sorry for the parents whose sons grow up to become idlers and lazy asses with the huge conceit that they are four-star generals. They have raised them this

139

way. There are no miracles, my friend. People say for a reason 'As you sow, so shall you reap.'"

Sometimes it could take Sam hours to express everything that had accrued in his mind and emotions. He shared his most interesting thoughts about his patients with Green Joe.

"The whore mother can't count on respect in old age. Of course, there is an unconditional love for parents, but in warped souls it often does not remain. It is replaced with pain, suffering, and heartache sown in childhood and sprouting like weeds through the personality and human nature. Love could be clogged with no confidence, neither in themselves nor in other people, and sometimes with hatred, and that's the worst. Nurtured and filled with these sort of feelings—they are bringing destruction and ugliness, decay of morals and flawed views. It not that the world and circumstances are changing around us; it's all about people. People are changing and their values are becoming more and more cynical and ugly with every generation. Unconditional love being reborn into something else, into some sophisticated dependency or unconscious imitation, and the worst cases are when this morbid love turns into mania. And again, whom to blame? At least the more diseases they bring here to our sessions, the fewer left out there."

Green Joe didn't argue since cactuses are not in the habit of arguing.

14

Anna could not be counted as any of the three types of Dr. Haley's patients, but she was no less lonely and lost. She had been a black sheep in their field. To Gina, Anna seemed to be really unhealthy, unlike the rest of the patients, who were just unhappy with their lives.

Anna, as always, came on time. Not earlier nor later—right on time. That day wasn't the exception, but she looked more lost than usual. Her hair was hidden under a cap. She was dressed in dirty jeans, a stretched T-shirt, and an unseasonably warm jacket. Anna lost weight, her face was haggard, dark circles under her eyes were too evident. She was shaking as if it was cold. She was trying to warm up, wrapping in her jacket.

"Hi Gina." Anna stood in the doorway, hesitating to enter. She finally made the effort, crossed the threshold and sat down on the couch.

"Good afternoon, Anna, how are you?" Gina said kindly, not looking up from her monitor. She was looking for wedding salons online. "The weather is so wonderful today, isn't it?"

Anna didn't answer.

Gina looked up but didn't recognize Anna. The woman who was sitting on the couch looked more like a homeless person with a terrible hangover. Gina got up from her desk and walked over to the couch where Anna was sitting. She was going to offer her coffee or water, but Gina really wanted to make sure that it was Anna and no one else. Anna raised her head and their eyes met. Gina felt her skin crawl, and she suddenly felt cold. It seemed that a huge, black cloud loomed over Anna's head. Gina felt as if it was somebody's shadow. A huge, black human shadow, heavy and dark. The shadow almost hugged Anna's body that was shaking from an imaginary cold. All of her being was crying for help. But at the same time, she knew that nobody could help her. And her fate was sealed. Gina stumbled backwards. She couldn't look away. She felt like something was pulling her into the abyss; she even felt dizzy.

"Hello Anna." The doctor's voice sounded like a life-saving signal during the unequal fight. Gina finally came around and returned to her desk. Sam stood at the open door of his office, waiting for Anna. After she came in, he closed the door.

"Please have a seat. Are you okay? Anything happened?" Sam tried to look in her eyes, but she hid them.

Anna silently sat down on the couch. She didn't take a figurine this time, didn't even look in that direction. She stared straight ahead for a few minutes. Then Anna raised her eyes and looked at the doctor. That was the first time Sam saw her "real" eyes, full of grief and pain, asking only one question: Why?

Sam didn't have an answer. He was looking at her not as his "special" patient, but as a friend who was in trouble, seeking help. But too late. In front of him on the couch there sat a woman, unhappy, resentful at fate, insanely tired but still a beautiful woman. Sam could hardly keep emotions from surging in him. He wanted to hug Anna, to offer his friendly shoulder, to give her the opportunity to cry. She always complained that she could not cry, could not allow weakness because she had to be strong; she couldn't allow herself to give up. The doctor was sincerely sorry that he hadn't met Anna in other circumstance. Maybe they could become friends, and he could better help her. But she was sitting on the couch in his office. She was weakened and miserable and sought the answer to just one question: Why? Anna turned to the window and started to speak.

"I can't help… It's too late... No chance… This disease leaves no chance for anybody, neither adult, nor a child… Just a few letters, but they sound like doom. They are doom... The AIDS…" The word suddenly fell from her lips and hung in the air. Terrible word. Doomed word. The word without hope. "I am... Baby... Nothing matters. Nothing makes sense." Anna bit her upper lip.

Sam missed a beat, his ears rang. His thought, *No, It's not possible. It's just a delusion. It's an echo of a sick imagination. But why?* But his intuition was screaming at him that it was too late. All that he could do at that moment was just try to comfort her. To take at least part of the burden of her grief on his shoulders. At least a part of what had happened or never happened to her. Sam forgot about all decencies, came to Anna, knelt down, and hugged her. She didn't resist. The shadow that was hanging over Anna covered Sam as well. He could feel her despair. The doctor tried to find the right words to ask her what happened and what she was talking about. But he could not utter a single word.

His heavy feeling of the impending misfortune, forgotten for a while, came back, but twice as strong. Sam's heart was pounding; it was hard for him to breathe. He tried to get himself together, to think of a question or to find an answer but couldn't find either.

143

His thoughts were frozen, unwilling to move. No chance to find a right word.

Anna tried to say something, but she was unable to gather letters into the right words. She was breathing irregularly, whispering under her breath. "I can't any more... I can't get back... Mommy... Mommy. I can't..." Suddenly Anna began to cry.

It was the first time Sam saw her cry. It was like a river raging in the bowels of a cliff. For many years, water sharpened stones, then punched its way out, and finally broke into a waterfall. Her crying was spilling over as if a high mountain river crashed on the sharp rocks below the cliff.

Anna snuggled into Sam's chest, continuing to cry harder. Soon her crying slowly turned into a low moan. Anna suddenly pulled back from the doctor's chest as if she remembered something. It seemed she calmed down. Sam could not understand how to behave and what to say to her. He remained silent. He wanted to absorb her tears and finally understand what tormented her, what was the true cause of her madness and if she was insane at all. Anna didn't utter a sound. Time had stopped, giving a chance to both.

"Thank you for everything," Anna said quietly, breaking the silence. "Now I got it... I'm not afraid anymore... I'm free." She turned to him. Sam didn't move. He met her gaze: It was clear and peaceful. "Thank you."

"Anna." He took her hand and squeezed it. His voice wavered but sounded soft as usual. "I really want to help you. I know one place where you and your child will be under good care. You should come with me, Anna. Believe me. Please for your own sake and for the sake of your baby. I can take you there right now if you let me. Please, Anna, please let me help you. Give me just one chance. I promise you'll never regret it. Anna, I promise, just one chance, please."

"Baby... Baby..." Anna spoke almost in a whisper.

Sam didn't take his eyes off her. He watched how her glazed-over gaze returned. Her dead look into the distance. Suddenly a shadow of a smile ran across her lips. Her gaze cleared again; her face was peaceful. The cloud that followed her had disappeared.

"Baby... It's all over... I'm free... I'm free..." Anna stood up abruptly, freed her arm, and confidently walked toward the door.

"Thank you, Dr. Haley. Thank you!" Without saying goodbye to Gina, Anna ran out into the hall right toward the stairs, not willing to wait for the elevator.

Sam did not come around for a while. He didn't understand what Anna meant. He wanted to run after her, to stop her, to try to calm her down and persuade her to go with him to the Five Stars clinic. He would like to talk to her again, not as a doctor but as a friend. But he couldn't move; his body became numb.

It seemed to him that time had stopped and leaned on his chest, pushing hard with disturbing presentiment. He needed to help her; he needed to arrange for her to meet with the professor. If it proved necessary, he was ready to enlist the help of an officer. He would just have to find the piece of paper with his phone number, which the professor gave him last time.

Suddenly Sam heard a shrill sound and a metallic screech from somewhere far away and it brought him back to reality. He jumped to the window and saw that an accident had occurred on the highway. He ran out of his room, but stopped when he saw Gina. He said to her quickly, slightly out of breath, "There is an accident on the highway; could you please check what happened. Gina, I just..." Sam did not finish.

"Accident? Oh Lord!" Gina jumped up and ran toward the front door. "I'll be right back."

Sam waited for Gina, walking around the room. He was asking himself why he didn't go himself— everything would be clear already. Subconsciously, he was waiting for Gina's return with fear. He was afraid it was Anna right there in one of those cars. He was scared. He couldn't explain his feelings about her, but emotions overwhelmed him; he was genuinely worried for her. Finally, he heard quick steps. Gina knocked and opened the door.

"Oh, Dr. Haley, what nonsense!" She was out of breath. "One guy was chasing another guy; people said that first guy had caught the other one with his wife. And now, oh what nonsense, they both have been taken away in an ambulance. They both are just idiots!"

"Yeah, you're right! They both are just idiots!" Sam laughed. "Thank you, Gina."

Sam felt better. He calmed down and smiled at his own stupidity. Why would he think it was Anna? She must be okay.

Dr. Haley thought that tears were kind of a good sign in Anna's case. Finally, she was able to cry out everything that had been sitting inside of her. He decided that she had begun trust him a little more. However, the disturbing feeling had not receded. Something had got his attention for a moment, then something else grabbed his thoughts, and then more and more different things were taking him over.

15

The hanging swing creaked, swaying in the wind. It was cloudy and wet after yesterday's rain but still warm enough for a summer outfit. The humid air did not allow anyone to breathe in fully, making it impossible to get enough oxygen, turning every motion sleepy and clumsy. The playground was deserted at that time. She specifically chose a time when there was almost nobody around, so no one would pester her with stupid, polite questions. She didn't want to get any attention or answer any question. They went to the main playground as they always did. The woman took her child in her arms and headed to the swings. She swung the creaking swing for 10 minutes, but both got tired of the sound soon. She stopped the swing and helped her kid to come down and they both ran to the bright red slide. That happened rarely when the mother and her child both were in a great mood at the same time. It was almost a ritual, twice a month, driving her kid to the park. And always first the swing, then the slide, and finally she bought ice cream or cotton candy.

Usually they had quite a lot of fun. And that day was supposed to be similar to dozens of others. Suddenly, the child screamed loudly and started crying right after the first trip down the slide. Blood flowed over the child's leg. The woman didn't realize immediately what had happened. She grabbed the kid and ran to the restroom to wash the wound. Another mother walking nearby with her children watched the incident; she quickly took her children to her car and called 911. The ambulance and the police arrived quickly. The woman took her poor child out of the restroom. The cuts were deep; she could not stop the bleeding. The emergency medical technician treated the wound and insisted they proceed to the hospital. The woman didn't have any energy to argue. She had a clear understanding that her child needed professional medical help. She got into her car and drove behind the ambulance, trying to control herself. The police had inspected the slide and found the pieces of thin, almost invisible, but sharp glass, deliberately fixed on it with adhesive and all wet from blood. Someone wanted to hurt the kids. The scene was roped off for further examination. All glass pieces were collected and sent for analysis.

The emergency room of the municipal hospital was crowded. But they didn't have to wait long. The child was placed in a private room.

The nurses ran around the child, gathering everything necessary to run all the tests; then they finally left them alone. The mother sat on the chair next to the bed, covering her face with her hands. Tears slowly rolled down, making her hands wet.

The child was lying on the bed, out of strength to cry; the wounds on the child's leg ached despite the painkillers. A nurse came in hurriedly, gave some paperwork to the mother to sign. She signed without even looking at it.

They stayed in the hospital for a few hours. The painkillers kicked in and the poor little thing fell asleep. The mother fell asleep sitting in a chair. A couple of hours later, the nurse woke her up, asking in a whisper for her to follow. She followed nurse to another separate room, which looked like a room for bad news. A small, windowless room with dim light so as not to clearly see the eyes of the ones who were doomed to suffering or going through irreparable loss. A physician stood next to the table; he offered her a seat and asked how she was feeling. She sat down on the uncomfortable chair. The doctor sat down on a chair opposite and moved the folder with paperwork closer. He tried not to look at her, instead staring at the test results; then finally he raised his head and met her tired eyes. He paused for another minute and then started to speak quietly.

"We are not sure... We can't say anything for 100 percent as of today. It takes time and we would need to observe your child, but ... I'm sorry ma'am, but..." He paused, looked to the papers and continued. "The glass collected from the slide on the playground, the one that wounded your baby ... there was not only your child's blood on it. We have found somebody else's fresh blood. I am sorry..." He paused again as if trying to squeeze out the next word. "Unfortunately, this blood is a fresh sample, and it's HIV-positive. We are currently not able to run the final tests and find out if your child has been infected. We have to wait. The incubation period ranges from two to four weeks to three months on average. That means we'll be able to diagnose only after a few weeks. I'm so sorry, ma'am." He paused and lowered his head, staring at the stack of papers in the folder.

She sat silently and looked straight ahead. Unexpected terrible news made her dizzy. Everything swam in her eyes. She held the table with both hands, trying to resist and not fall off the chair. The mother had ceased to understand where she was and what was happening; she looked straight at the doctor, but did not see him. She whispered under her breath, "How come? Why? Why?" The tears flowed over her face. It seemed that she grew old in one second. The doctor who brought her the evil news would never forget her face. That's what real grief, impending doom, and helplessness look like.

The woman got up from the table, went to the wall, and leaned forehead on the cool surface. The air grill was directly above her head. She raised her head, putting her face to the cold air, then leaned her back to the wall, slowly sliding to the floor.

She laughed aloud, then tore the crucifix off her neck and threw it to the side. The laugh turned into hysterics. No one dared to come to her. Nobody tried to calm her, to tell her everything would be fine and they still had a chance. She sat hiding her face in hands. The hysteria came down slightly and turned to quiet crying. God, faith, hope—these words finally ceased to exist for her in that moment.

She sat there for half an hour. Her solitude was interrupted by the same physician who recently talked to her. "Ma'am the police have arrived; they want to ask you a few questions. If you don't mind."

She raised her face. Her eyes expressed nothing; she stared into the distance. She made an effort and returned to her seat at the table. An officer came in. His head was densely covered with grey hair. The officer held two cups with steam coming out of them and a folder with papers under his arm.

"Would you like some coffee, ma'am?" he asked quietly

"Yes, thank you." She slowly came around and began to realize what was happening.

"Ma'am, I'm sorry." The officer tried to speak as gently as possible. "There is still hope. Don't give up." He put the mug with coffee to her right. She glanced at the steam rising above the drink. "Do you often go on that playground? Maybe you have noticed something unusual today? Someone nearby? He had to be somewhere close to the slide. Try to remember if you've seen anybody."

"No, I mean yes, often, but nothing unusual. Everything was as always, first swing, then slide, everything as usual." She took a sip and put the mug back on the table, aligning it with the wet trail on the table.

"Ma'am," he looked right at her but it seemed she didn't see him, "the physician who examined your child told us that he found traces of injuries on the baby's body. Can you explain them?"

"I am... Baby... I love my child. This baby is all that I have." Her voice changed, became cold and distant. Her skin crawled and her gaze drowned in emptiness.

"Ma'am, please try to concentrate and answer the question." The officer was polite and calm. "The child is missing two fingers on the left hand. What happened? We found no records of the incident. Where did the burns on the baby's back come from? Some of them are quite fresh, as well as the wounds on the legs. When was the last time you took your child to the pediatrician? Ma'am, can you hear me?" He waved his hand in front of her face, but she didn't respond.

The officer tried to stay impartial and calm, but it was difficult. He clearly understood that she was crippling her own child. He had faced similar cases before in his career. He could recognize what was going on easily.

"I'm afraid we have to leave the child in the hospital for a while. The baby needs to stay under the supervision of a physician. Ma'am, can you hear me? Do you understand what I'm saying? You can be deprived of parental rights. They can take you from your child."

"No! Why?" She woke up for a second. "No! My baby is all that I have." Her eyes showed tears. Her gaze darted around the room. She trembled and couldn't understand what this officer wanted from her. Why she couldn't take her baby home? She was the mother and she was taking care of her child as well as she could; she was trying her best.

"Ma'am, it would be better for the baby, as of now." The officer felt sorry for her. He paused for a few minutes, then got up and left the room.

He came back five minutes later. She still was sitting in the same place, and her wet eyes were staring in the distance. The officer took his seat and continued quietly, "I'd like you to meet someone. This is important; this person will be able to help you and your baby. Whatever I do for you would be under my personal responsibility. Please believe me. I am trying to help you and wish nothing but happiness for you and your child."

"My baby. You can't…" She was crying. "I can't. Please. That's all that I have."

"Ma'am, you'd better go home now. I have arranged a meeting for tomorrow." He helped her to get up. "Don't worry about your child; the nurse will take care of everything. We will help you if you agree to some terms. The most important is that you'll be able to stay with your child. But you would have to move." The officer held her arm and spoke as they walked to the exit. "Tomorrow you'll learn everything. He will help you. I'll pick you up, and we'll go to him. Please get all necessities packed. I'll bring your child with me, and we'll all go together. It's okay, ma'am, everything will be fine."

The officer asked the patrol car driver to give her a ride home. She was not able to drive. Her mind couldn't understand what she did wrong, why they wanted to take away her child. It would be the first night she slept alone without her baby since she gave birth. She could not fall asleep. She packed everything. She thought that she could hear her baby crying and calling for her, and she jumped up and ran to the empty bedroom. She couldn't find the baby in the crib and at first was frightened, but then remembered what happened and starting crying. After a while, she calmed down, and then everything started all over again, until she finally got tired and fell asleep in the living room on the small couch.

The next morning, her life would change forever.

16

Gina didn't get a chance to talk to Sam on Monday. After his meeting with Anna, Dr. Haley canceled all appointments and asked Gina not to disturb him for the rest of the day. Gina was hoping to snatch a moment that day and not delay longer. The same Monday morning, Sam had notified her that he was going to be out of town from Wednesday until the end of the week. Gina was short on time; she had to give notice of her resignation two weeks prior, and then with a quiet conscience, deal with preparations for her wedding. Sam wasn't long in coming; he greeted Gina and slipped into his office. She poured him a cup of coffee and knocked on his door.

"Come in," Sam sat at his desk, working on some papers. Gina put his cup at its usual place and started to speak timidly.

"Hey, I need to talk to you about something personal."

"Sure. What happened?" Sam stared at Gina with surprise.

It was the first time Gina tried to talk to him about something personal in the five years they had been working together. Their relationship was strictly business, and she always kept her personal matters separate. She never even asked permission to leave early. She always notified him about her vacations in writing a couple months prior to her planned absences. Gina had never been late, and if it was necessary, she could stay late; she always performed all responsibilities accurately. She was the kind of assistant any doctor could only dream of.

"Nothing, I am just going to get married soon… And…"

"Oh, congratulations!" Sam got up, came out from behind his desk and hugged Gina. "I hope your partner understands in full how lucky he is!" Sam was genuinely happy for her.

"Thank you, Dr. Haley. I'll send you an invitation later; they are not ready yet. We are still— well, it doesn't matter." Gina faltered. "Dr. Haley, unfortunately, I have to quit. Immediately after the wedding, me and my husband, we're going to move to his hometown; it's in another state. So … I'd like to inform you about it in advance." Gina blurted out everything quickly and froze, waiting for his answer.

"Hmm… A bit of a surprise." Sam was lost in thought for a second. "And how soon are you going to leave?"

"In two weeks. That's the plan, but if you need more time, then I'm certainly not going to rush. I understand it would take time to hire someone else."

"No, no. I think I'll be fine." Sam smiled conspiratorially.

"Do you want me to post an ad online or maybe you have someone in mind? I could ask my friends if someone is looking for a job."

"Thank you, Gina. Don't worry. I'll figure it out." He smiled and got back to his papers.

Gina shrugged and went back to her desk. She had a strange feeling of anxiety for the doctor. He had never done any of the administrative tasks, always trusting Gina in full. But she had decided she didn't want to think about anything other than her wedding. She still had a lot to do. Matthew relied on Gina and

155

allowed her to choose all necessary trifles. Gina was supported by his mother, and they surprisingly had a lot of similar ideas and their tastes were identical. They were easygoing with each other and could spend hours shopping for table linens and all other important stuff for the event.

Sam finally had been left on his own. He began to search for information about Anna. He worried about her more after she had canceled her appointment for the current week and the following one as well. *Maybe she went on vacation, just to get away from it all*, Sam thought. It seemed to him that Anna's absence meant significant advancement in her state since her last visit.

He thought that she finally had relaxed a bit. But what did she mean by saying the scary word "AIDS"? The word wouldn't leave Sam's head, making him even more worried.

"Is it possible? No! It's not! She would tell me, or somehow make it clear. This is not just a common cold. This disease requires a diagnosis and does not exhibit primary symptoms earlier than a few weeks after infection. I saw her just a week ago and she looked quite normal for her state. What could happen during a week, not even for a week, over the weekend, just a few days!" As usual, Sam addressed his questions to Green Joe. And as usual, he didn't get any answer.

He continued to dig in the papers from her folder. There was not enough information, only a copy of her driver's license and some data about her place of work and phone number. He tried to dial several times but no one answered. He tried to verify the address on her license, but to no avail. He called her work but was told that Anna had resigned the day before, explaining her instant decision was family reasons. This news finally convinced Sam that something serious had happened to her. But he couldn't imagine what.

Sam was thinking about calling the police, but what would he say? Less than 24 hours had passed since their last meeting. And how he would explain his concerns? His intuition wouldn't play as argument. And her destructive thoughts about AIDS and the fact that she burst into tears and ran away were quite normal, considering her diagnosis. No one would take him seriously. He could only wait.

He decided to leave unsuccessful attempts for a while and focused on folders that he had brought from Five Stars. The professor gave him a few cases to read as promised. And he took his word that he would return them unharmed and would keep everything he read confidential. A couple folders were cases of deep postpartum depression with uncontrolled hysterics, but easily recoverable. The next few folders dealt with severe mental disorders.

Sam read the medical histories of poor women and their unfortunate children. Each story was a small life that the professor had lived through along with the patients. Every case was an individual world with its own drama, small victories, and for the most part, a happy ending—or rather, the beginning of a new life.

January 15, 1989

Mother's name: Milla Iveen

Age: 34

Preliminary Diagnose: Persecutory delusion / advanced stage

The main delusion fear: afraid that someone will take her child away from her. Ran away from home a year and a half ago. Had been wandering with her daughter through the forest. Been eating poorly. Avoided people.

The child: Chris Iveen, a girl

Age: 9

Child's state upon arriving: child exhausted, extensive sores all over the body, probably infected. Hardly ever says a word, delusional. Walks with difficulty. Depressed, afraid of people. As per father's words: The girl was subjected to mental and physical pressure from the mother's side for several years before they escaped.

He carefully read all papers stacked in the folder. Sam found the methods of the professor, though not traditional, humane and effective. The last page of the folder informed that the happy family was discharged into the world on March 15, 1995. Supervisor: Emma. Then some weekly notes on checking. Then monthly notes, quarterly, and final note "removed from further observation."

One of the families successfully returned to the big world from the town. Sam wondered what they could have been doing. He thought that maybe he had met some of these people. Maybe one of them lived next door or used to have lunch at the same café as he usually did. Or maybe some of them went to his favorite deli store to get a sandwich. It could be. He spent the rest of the day going through the Five Stars folders he had at his desk. Sam couldn't leave his thoughts, trying to make a final decision and as usual asking Green Joe.

"Maybe this is my way? And Gina getting married and leaving me right on time. I won't even need to fire her and explain anything in case I accept the professor's offer. Maybe the professor is right and I am made to go this way."

Anri had offered Sam the position of his assistant last Sunday evening, right before Sam left Five Stars—not leaving him an opportunity to reject the offer without thinking first. And now Sam was trying to decide, comparing the yes and no columns. He thought that actually the professor was right when saying that Sam had nothing in the big city to hold him. No family, no best friends, even his Auntie Darrel had left forever. And regarding his voluntary mentees, he thought he would be able to see them by going to the city from time to time until they finally recovered. Sam sat in his office, thinking all day long. Time flew imperceptibly; it became dark outside the window. He turned on the desk lamp, and its light scattered across the ceiling, leaving everything around to languish in the shadows.

Sam was a little tired and leaned back in his chair, remembering Anna. He started to think about her swan-like neck, mysterious smile, so bright and pure. He only once saw her like that, in a good mood without a single hint of the disease. That day she came in for a session wearing a light summer dress with blue flowers and wasn't wrapped in a warm sweater, as usually happened. She was light and free as a feather in the wind; they had talked about love. And Anna spoke so calmly, so serenely. Sam remembered their conversation well.

Anna said that true love doesn't need proof with loud actions. Passion is the thing that squeezes out all juices, moving people to unpredictable extremes. Love is much smarter and fine-minded. Love doesn't need dramatic performances; it doesn't need triumphant fanfare as well. It requires quite different things. The main requirement for love is daily patience, continuous participation, care, and all these require much more strength and endurance than any of the labors of Hercules.

Love cannot be proven by means of madness. Love is much smarter. It always asks to give her the most important and valuable thing. The thing that is given only once and forever. Love would require her whole life in order to prove her dedication. And if your love is mutual, you are lucky, as it will give you the equivalent gift back. It will give you another life, the life of your beloved. But if your love is unhappy, then nothing will ever replace the life you gave away. This place will remain empty forever. Like a huge, black, bottomless hole that will suck everything out of you: youth, beauty, and health. And no matter how much alcohol you pour into this hole, no matter how many expensive and useless things you throw into this black endlessness, the black hole will never fill up; it will never heal. It will remain the same emptiness. And only time will gradually fill this emptiness with its magic sand. And one day you'll see that the hole has a bottom. But it will be too late, and you'll realize that the hole has turned into a grave. And soon your lifeless body in a wooden box will be dropped down there. You have to be careful with love. Don't give it to anybody; otherwise you run the risk of losing your life, most likely forever.

Sam had agreed with her. He remembered that day, how after her session he had two more patients and then went to the bar. He drank too much that night and still couldn't remember how he managed to get home. It was the seventh anniversary of his wife's death. He always went to the bar at that time of day for a couple drinks and after that went back to his lonely apartment and fell asleep in his cold bed.

That day he thought that Anna was right. Love takes your life. He gave away his own a long time before. Sam was lucky: He had another life gifted to him by his wife. But by dying, she took both their lives and left in his soul a huge hole that Sam was never able to fill. He realized he was attracted to and at the same time scared of Anna, because she reminded him of his wife in those hard times when she was fading. He wasn't attentive enough to her needs, but he wouldn't ever forget the way she looked at him. It was the same stony gaze that now forced his body to be numb and his mind to race.

And he suddenly felt scared that he would never see Anna. He drove the bad thoughts away and forced his intuition to shut up. Sam decided that tomorrow, in return for his final agreement, he would ask the professor to help him find Anna and to place her with the child for treatment in the town, although at first, they both would have to go through the buildings, but that was okay—it would be temporary. Anri's methods were effective, and it wouldn't take long for Anna to recover. This thought calmed Sam down, and he started preparations for the future changes.

He still had to refer all his patients to his colleagues. He didn't care to whom exactly; in the end, the patient had the right to choose or to change the doctor. It was necessary to inform the office building management about his lease agreement termination and also to take care of his apartment. Sam was short on time: only two weeks, a deadline he had agreed on. That would be enough time for him to take care of all outstanding issues. He came home around midnight and, without taking a shower, fell into bed and got lost in a deep sleep.

The alarm rang a minute later after Sam fell asleep—or so it seemed to him. He could not open his eyes and forced himself to get out of bed by thinking of hot coffee and Melinda's delicious croissants. Sam quickly brought himself to order, packed all the necessary things for a few days, and went to Five Stars. The road had become familiar as much as the fellowship with the odd man from the gas station. Sam guessed the guy was one of the ex-residents of the town.

"Good morning, Professor!" Sam got out of his car, parked at the same place as last time. The weather was wonderful; the breeze was invigorating with its freshness. Anri was waiting for Sam on the porch of the main house, dressed as always in a beautiful dressing gown over a shirt and trousers.

"Good morning, Dr. Haley!" The professor was a little nervous. "I must admit I am glad to see you. Does this mean you decided to accept my offer?" He stared at Sam with a direct, inquiring gaze.

"Exactly." Sam lit a cigarette, leaning on the railing of the porch. "I think you were right in saying that I have nothing but work. So, if I'm really living to work, I want to be ultimately useful."

"I dare to correct you, my friend. Here it ceases to be work and becomes a way of life. It becomes the life itself."

"Yes, that's what I meant." Sam didn't want to finish his cigarette and threw it away. "Can I hope for a fresh, delicious cup of coffee made by Melinda?" He smiled.

"Oh, of course! Forgive my inhospitality. Melinda has served our breakfast already and is waiting for us." The professor opened the door with courtesy, let Sam go ahead, and entered the house after him.

Melinda had already set out breakfast. As always, there were fresh pastries and some spreads. The smell of coffee managed to break through the closed kitchen doors and played with the anticipation. Anri invited Sam to take his usual place at the table and sat himself. Sam had the impression the professor had lost weight in just a week. His dressing gown, which usually fit him perfectly, was hanging on him as if Anri had overestimated a couple of sizes when buying it. Sam also noticed that the professor was talking a little quieter than usual, pausing more often to catch his breath. By all signs, the disease has progressed, but Anri didn't want to talk about it, and Sam didn't dare ask.

"We would have to do a lot within the next few weeks. As much as usually requires at least a few years." The professor was speaking seriously and was a little excited. "But you'll always have Lola and Isabelle, Emma and Ray around, and all the others will render you all possible assistance, but it is important to understand," Anri paused meaningfully and looked into Sam's eyes, "it is important to understand you'll have to bear the main responsibility, and they all, despite their years of experience, will look to you to give them answers and instructions. They'll be your support, they'll be your family, but you'll always be the head of this family. The guests come and go, not all, but the majority, and the staff—your family—will remain here forever. That is their choice. The main rule, Doctor, you should also remember from now on is don't force anyone to stay who wants to leave, and don't force anyone to leave if they want to stay. Even if, in your opinion, they are ready to go. Some need more time— please remember this. The only exception is the building with five stars. All other people are free. The same free as you and me, my friend, and it is important to understand it and accept this fact."

The kitchen door opened. Melinda entered the dining room carrying a tray with a coffee pot on it. "Good morning, Dr. Haley." She stopped near Sam, put the tray on the table and gave the doctor her hand.

"Good morning, Melinda." The doctor was surprised and therefore a bit confused, but did not show it. He smiled and gently shook Melinda's hand. "I missed your delicious coffee and croissants." Sam thought Melinda must be at least 10 years older than he was. But despite her age, she seemed childlike at times.

"I hope this is not the only reason you are here." Melinda smiled, her look softened; she was no longer afraid of the doctor, realizing that he would soon take the place of the professor and they would have to live under the same roof.

Breakfast dragged on for a long time. To save time, both agreed to smoke on the way to the buildings and not on the balcony.

"Today we will visit the building with five stars." The professor drove slower than usual. "There are no guests in that building, there are patients only, because they are unable to move freely even in the building and hardly have a chance for a free life even in our town.

"How are you feeling, Professor?" Sam asked suddenly.

"I'm fine, my friend, don't worry. But thank you for asking."

They drove to the buildings. As always, first they went to the main building where they were met by Lola with her daily report and questions about some current issues. After they were done with Lola, they went up to the office where the professor took a couple of scribbled notepads and made some notes on the papers lying on his desk. Then Anri and Sam went back down and headed to the building with five large stars on the front door.

The professor was coughing longer and stronger than usual. After each attack, he looked more and more tired, quickly hiding his handkerchief in his pants pocket. But Sam had noticed the red spots on it anyway. When they came to the door of the building with five stars, he stopped and asked Anri, "How long?"

The professor understood his question, smiled, and said after he caught his breath from walking, "I don't know, my friend, but I feel that time is slipping away so fast. We need to hurry. I will try to be as brief as possible to explain my methods. I trust you, Dr. Haley, and I trust in your intuition; you'll be fine. Let's go."

It was light and cool in the lobby. The light was always on. The bright lights left dark marks on the ceiling, heating it constantly. To the right of the stairs there was a door to the attendant staff room. Anri and Sam went there first. There were several monitors, each fixed on the wall next to the desk. Sam remembered that the professor had told him about the video observation system for patients in the five stars building, citing the necessity of this measure for the welfare of patients and their families. He also mentioned an accident with one of the patients that took place a few years ago. No one still had figured out what actually happened. But after the incident, the professor ordered the installation of cameras in every room and the observation of particular patients. And especially to follow closely when patients received any kind of visitors. Even if they lived in the town.

Two persons sat at the desk, a man and a woman. Both had thin wedding rings glistening on their ring fingers. Apparently, they were husband and wife and most likely newlyweds. She was dark-skinned, tall and skinny with coarse facial features, high cheekbones, sunken cheeks, thin lips, and close-cropped black hair. Her name was Keisha. He was of average height, with incipient signs of a belly, gray, thinning hair, and a round face with plump lips. His name was Peter. A pair of opposites tightly attracted to each other. They gave the impression of a happy couple, at least it seemed so if you paid attention to the glances they gave each other every single minute. It seemed they couldn't stop looking at each other, couldn't get enough of each other.

After they all were done with greetings, Keisha took from the drawer a bunch of keys and handed them to the professor. Anri had already informed everybody that Sam was going to replace him soon. No one asked him about the reason; it was too clear for all of them as they had known the professor for years. Now everybody was looking at Sam with due respect and recognition. Anri took the bunch of keys, exchanged a few more words with Keisha and Peter, and along with Sam took the stairs to the second floor. Unlike the other buildings, the doors of the rooms of this building were locked and each had a small monitor next to it.

"Just another extra security measure," Anri said with a hint of an excuse, opening the first door from the right. He paused. "Here we are trying to help the poor little thing who was struck with postpartum psychosis with prolonged negative emotions in the background. Plus, she had inherited schizophrenia, but the disease had never showed a single sign and broke through only after delivery." The professor opened the door.

"Good morning, sweetheart. How are you feeling today?" Anri headed to the woman lying on the bed. She was more like a shadow of the once-blossoming and now quite withered woman.

"We are good. Thank you. We're looking to go for a walk." The shadow hugged a toy rabbit with painted eyes, nose, and mouth. "My baby didn't sleep well last night, and we are a little tired. I think the fresh air will bring us back to life." She spoke slowly, but confidently, as if she was really going for a walk, and this idea was reflected with a joyous echo in her trembling voice. But at the same time, the woman didn't move. She just lay on the bed, crumpling a toy in her hands. The brand-new soft, warm bed slippers stood next to bed. The chair was bolted to the floor. Everything on the chair—dressing gown, tracksuit, and some more things—were neatly folded. Sam noticed that the clothes and shoes were new and quite expensive with well-known brand tags.

"Have you eaten your breakfast today?" The professor walked over to the bed and gently sat on its edge. He furrowed his brows and continued in a tone parents usually use to portray discontent when talking to toddlers, "Who goes for a walk without having breakfast first? I am sure you'll spend a lot of time outside because the weather is wonderful today. Let me ask your maid to serve you breakfast. And after you're done with your meal, she'll help you dress for your walk." Anri held her hand. It was such a thin hand, almost transparent with bluish threads of thin veins.

She tried to raise her head and for a few seconds she succeeded. The doctor managed to see her face. It seemed familiar to him, but he couldn't remember her name. The professor talked to the woman for a while more, then patted her head, got up and they went out, locking the door behind.

Anri pulled out a card with her medical history, slipped it into the terminal and made a note. He returned everything back to its place and turned to Sam.

"Helen Cram. You must have recognized her."

"Exactly! Cram, God, I couldn't remember where I saw her." Sam frowned. "But she looks different. And what's she doing here? I remember the press wrote that doctors had found some rare disease right after she gave a birth to her daughter. And that she went to Switzerland for treatment."

"As you can see, Doctor, here is her Switzerland. And her disease is not that rare." The professor coughed. "Poor girl, she wanted to give her parents the boy grandchild they dreamed about. But she gave birth to a girl. Helen knows firsthand how it feels to be an unwelcome daughter when her parents dreamed of a son. Helen tried to prove to her parents that even being a girl she deserves their love no less than if she were born a boy. All her sports achievements just for the sake of earning the love of her parents. To satisfy the ambitions of her mother, who had once been a potential sports champion. But because of the pregnancy and family pressure, her mother had to leave sports. She had to go into coaching. But being a coach she never achieved anything worth attention. Her mom was a pretty mediocre coach of a team of amateurs. Helen tried so hard. She was so scared during whole her life. And finally, after delivery she had a hormonal shock and just failed at some point. And a mental breakdown followed shortly. Helen could never rely on support from her family. And she gave up. In the end, exhausted by fear and doubts, Helen's mind decided that it would be better and easier for her to live in another invented reality. So, here she is. In her reality, she's surrounded by loved ones and raising a beautiful baby boy. Her daughter in the real world, as far as I know, is growing up in the same Spartan conditions and traditions. Poor child. But here I am powerless. The girl was legally adopted by Helen's mother. The baby has a guardian whose ambitions have not been realized yet. There are some people who never realize their lessons from life. They are so blind in their stupid stubbornness. It's not enough for her that she lost her daughter and her

169

husband; he just could not stand the shock and died of a heart attack. Now she'll finish off Helen's child, the same way she finished off her own before." The professor eyes became wet. "What a pity that there is no law prohibiting harming children this way. Mutilation of soul harms no less than any physical wound, and in contrast to many physical disorders, a soul wound can never be recovered from fully."

The professor paused. It took him a few minutes to catch his breath, and he continued with the explanation of treatment methods and details of the disease affecting Helen and others like her. Sam listened carefully, trying not to miss a single detail and recommendation. He tried to understand the professor's way of thinking and logic because his methods were more than effective, but not always traditional. When they finished discussing Helen's case, they went to the next door. Anri took the card from plastic pocket fixed on the wall over the door and slid it through the terminal.

"Patient: Angelica Grey." The professor returned card to its place. "Diagnosis: Jerusalem syndrome first type."

They entered the room. The woman sat on her knees at the window and her whole being was drawn to the sky outside the barred window. She was waiting for something, and in this expectation, she was spending long hours of her existence.

"Good morning, Angelica." The professor walked quietly, almost soundlessly. "How are you doing today?"

"Oh, it's you." The woman turned around. Half of her wrinkled face was covered with disheveled hair.

Her thin body was dressed in a robe hastily draped over her, as if she were in a hurry when wearing it. Her gaze was excited, full of enthusiasm and hope. The way young girls usually look at their idols.

"He said he'll be back soon. I should not miss. Last time I missed the moment, but not today. I'll wait for him here. He will come. He promised." She spoke in a voice that was more like a hoarse whisper.

"Of course, he'll come, but not from this side." Anri put his hand on her shoulder. "Angelica, he'll walk in the door. If you want, I'll ask the nurse to wake you up before he comes. You need to rest." The professor spoke slowly. Only now Sam noticed that the woman's hands were shaking.

"No!" she cried. "He'll come down from heaven! Why are you lying to me? You are deceiving me again! I got you! He always comes through the window! Because it's more convenient and easier for him!"

"Angelica, you should get some rest. Otherwise, I'll ask him not to come tonight and tomorrow also. Or I'll forbid him to come to you till you get enough rest and sleep. The nurse will bring you medication; please be so kind as to take the pill on your own." He turned to the doctor and the rest of the words sounded quieter and were addressed only to him, although the woman was not interested in their conversation. "I don't want to give her injections, as long as the pills working. It keeps her mind clearer, and she is able to enjoy her rare minutes of happiness when her son comes to visit."

"No! You cannot order him!" The woman was frustrated with what she just heard.

"I can't order, but I can ask." The professor spoke quietly.

"It is cruel!" she croaked.

"Get some rest, Angelica. He won't be happy to see you in such a state. You know how much he loves you and how much he cares. You need to sleep, then the nurse will help you brush your hair. Let him see you happy. He deserves it." The professor came closer to her and spoke all this slowly, clearly pronouncing every word.

"Maybe you're right." She lowered her head and stared at the floor. "Just promise me that you'll wake me up on time, please." Her voice had changed. No more excitement, only overwhelming sadness and fear.

"I promise you, the nurse will wake you up and help you look better. Come on, you need to get some rest." Anri took her by the arm and helped to the bed. She looked haggard. Her red eyes with black circles under them showed the deadly fatigue caused by her endless vigils.

"Just don't deceive me, please," Angelica whispered, barely audible. "Don't deceive."

The professor helped her get on the bed. Sam opened the door and they left.

"Her son is 25 now. He forgave his mother. He comes to visit her pretty often, knowing that she lives only when she sees him." The professor paused. He looked at Sam, then nodded to himself as if he still needed to get his own permission to continue. "But for her, he is the Messiah who ascended to heaven and returned to our world. Angelica crucified her son when he was about five years old. The boy nearly bled to death, but managed to survive. Their dog saved his life.

172

She sensed the baby was in trouble, even though his mother was around. The dog's loud, incessant barking attracted the attention of neighbors, and suspecting something was wrong, they called the police. After several vain attempts to reach Angelica, the door was broken down. The boy was found in a closet. The door was nailed shut. There was almost no air left to breathe. Angelica was almost in a trance caused by hunger and dramatic exacerbation of her disease. She was sitting, waiting for her son to ascend to heaven. And the boy was dying in a tightly-closed closet just next to her. I still don't understand how he survived. Very strong kid."

"And where was his father? Or anybody? Family?"

"Angelica lived in the city alone. She was raped and she found a religious shelter. But it turned out she was pregnant. And her injured psyche finally failed. Angelica came up with her own version of the situation. She convinced herself that it was immaculate conception and soon she was going to give a birth to the Messiah."

"Jesus was 33 when he was crucified; her son was only five. This was illogical if she followed the biblical story. He was too young."

"My dear friend, don't try to find logic in the actions of a sick person. It's not there and it never has been there! Angelica is sick. The disease had become ingrained into her mind so deeply that I'm afraid it will stay there for the rest of her days. From the moment she gave birth until she committed the crucifixion, Angelica was waiting for when her son would hear the call of his heavenly father. And she said the same thing to her boy all his life, promising to let him go. At some point, the child decided it was a game and if he played along with the mother, she would let him go as she promised. And he once said that his father spoke to him. He was just a little child; he couldn't imagine that by words 'to let him go' she meant to let him go to his father in heaven."

"Poor kid." Sam had put himself in the place of the boy for a moment and was horrified. A sense of pain and despair pierced his soul; he saw himself as a little boy in the locked closet, bleeding out with no hope for salvation. And the one who was supposed to take care of him and protect him instead betrayed him and locked him there to die alone in the dark. The professor noticed Sam's state.

"You feel everything, Sam. That's good. Otherwise it is impossible to help some of them. At first it will be hard, but you'll get used to it. The feelings of children who have suffered at the hands of the closest person on the planet, they help me not to give up and instead take care of them for so many years. But don't let them get too close to your heart; otherwise, it won't survive for long." Anri smiled and they continued to see patients.

Next door, the same plastic card. Mildred: 38 years old. Diagnosis: Capgras delusion.

"She saw the messenger of Satan in her own child. In the end she tried to burn the kid. One more miracle, the child managed to survive." Anri paused to catch his breath. It became hard to speak. And every other pause was longer than the previous one. He wiped his forehead with a handkerchief and continued. "The girl was 13 years old. This number finally drove her

174

mother crazy. She nailed shut the door of her daughter's room, poured gasoline over it and set it on fire one night. Mildred's husband worked a lot and didn't pay attention to the signs of her disease. He thought she was just tired from her daily routine like any other housewife. And their daughter had just become a teenager and that was the reason Mildred sometimes called her a demon or devil, so he thought it was fine. And meanwhile the disease was progressing and Mildred finally crossed the line."

"What the—" Sam wanted to say something, but suddenly stopped and wiped his mouth with his hand as if it were dirty.

"Mildred's husband died in the fire rescuing the child. The daughter is still recovering, but we already transferred her to the town with one of the families. The girl is learning to live again. She is learning to walk, to talk, to smile, but the nightmares will not recede soon. Maybe they will never leave. We don't talk to her about her parents yet. But we will work on it. We will do our best to help her. She won't pull the burden of hatred and resentment through all her life. She will forgive her mother eventually; she will forgive her. Although that will be difficult, almost impossible. But we will help her."

They visited one room after another, floor by floor. Each room had a hopelessly sick woman who had reflected her disease in a traumatized child's soul. The professor described the diseases and the history of the patients, trying not to miss any small detail, focusing on emotions. In his opinion, emotions hid a lot of questions, and most important, they could help him find the answer for the main question: Why did the women give up and succumb to the disease, leaving no way back?

Sam listened to every history, passing it through himself. He plunged into the world of the children's helplessness and fears, and felt disappointment in the most important person on Earth: a mother. Despair and pain filled his chest, pulled out his heart to break it into small pieces, and threw them out over the abyss. He began to shiver from time to time and sometimes cold sweat appeared. They finally came out of the last room. The professor looked at Sam with understanding.

"Too much for one day. But what can I do? We are too short on time."

They returned to the main house and went to their rooms to rest before dinner. It was necessary for both Sam and Anri to be alone for some time. Sam had to reflect on everything seen and heard. Anri had to ponder and highlight the most important, most necessary things. The details that should not be missed in any case as they could become lodestars for Sam to help him navigate in the dark kingdom of lost souls.

17

The professor went down to the living room first. The doctor joined him 10 minutes later. They both were tired and hungry.

"How about a glass of wine, Dr. Haley?" the professor offered unexpectedly. "Alcohol is not in my rules, but sometimes it is necessary."

"Well, if you twist my arm!" Sam needed to relax.

The professor went to the wall mirror and carefully pulled the frame of the second mirror from the left. A small wine rack was hidden behind the mirror. Anri took a look at the bottles and finally chose one. It was Gevrey Chambertin 1976.

"As far as I know, Melinda is cooking beef tonight. So this wine will fit right in."

"I don't have an iota of doubt in your choice," the doctor replied wearily.

Finally, Melinda invited them both to take their places at the table.

It was warm and cozy in the dining room. Melinda had served snacks and continued to conjure in the kitchen over the main course. Anri uncorked the bottle and poured a dark red wine into the glasses.

"Do you know, my friend, that Gevrey Chambertin was the favorite wine of the most famous Corsican known in history under the name of Napoleon?"

"I confess, Professor, I'm not a wine connoisseur. Especially the expensive ones."

"I wouldn't say this wine is expensive. But not the essence. So, according to some sources, the convoy with this wine followed the emperor in all his campaigns. Although some, also quite reliable sources, say that Napoleon had no clue about wine quality and the proper way of choosing it. He drank this sort of wine because once in the camp one soldier highly praised this wine, saying it cures all diseases, and its taste is divine. But not only Napoleon loved this sort of wine. The great Russian poet Pushkin loved this wine as well. I read about it somewhere, and according to rumors, Pushkin paid a small fortune for it, sometimes even falling into debt. But you know all these could be just fake gossip to sell the wine more."

"A wine with a story. Everything in this world has its own story. Even the harsh vinous liquid, the name of which, most likely, I won't even remember." Sam drank the wine and it seemed to him no better or worse than any other he had tried before. But the beef surpassed all expectations. Melinda did her best for the feast. The doctor had never tasted such tender, juicy meat, moderately seasoned, moderately salted, moderately roasted. Melinda outdid herself. The dish was a true masterpiece.

"What would you say of the proposal to spend all day tomorrow in the archive, Doctor?"

"Please call me Sam. I'll be grateful for that. About the archive. Yes, sure, why not."

"No problem, Sam. You can call me Anri if you want. The name is just the name." The professor smiled. "So, I just thought that it would be good for you to take a look at some cases. There may be some questions that only I can clarify. So, it is better not to leave for later. Because you never know what will happen tomorrow. If it is going to happen at all."

Melinda had tried to please the culinary tastes of both and had prepared a couple of different sauces and side dishes. Sam preferred hot and spicy sauces, and the professor enjoyed mild with sour. Both were happy with the dinner, which couldn't fail to please Melinda. She was one of those who knew about the professor's illness, but did not show that she knew. Every day she tried to brighten up the professor's life, at least through her cooking skills; unfortunately, she wasn't able to do anything else.

If only she could give away her own life and it could have saved Anri from certain death; she wouldn't hesitate to cut a deal even with the devil himself. Melinda loved her "Angel," considered him her father. It was hard to resist the emotions, but the professor would not be happy to see either tears or lamentations. She had to keep everything rolling in a usual manner. The only thing that changed was that she became more attentive and caring, trying to please him better in everything.

After dinner, it was decided to go to bed without further ado and late-night conversations. The day was long and uneasy. Any kind of physical exertion became harder for the professor every day, although he was carefully hiding that fact. He needed more time to recover his energy. And Sam surrendered to the alcohol mixed with fatigue and needed to rest and get his thoughts in order. They went to their rooms, wishing each other a good sleep and agreed to meet the next morning, no later than seven o'clock, in the dining room.

Anri took pain meds with sleeping pills and quickly fell asleep. Sam couldn't let go of the feeling of anxiety and the feeling of the constant presence of someone unknown in his room. The thoughts about Anna came back. Her sudden disappearance did not bode well. The next day, he was going to ask the professor to help him to find her. He could get help from his friend, the officer. It would make everything easier. Sam finally surrendered to Morpheus and fell into a restless sweaty abyss of dreams. He saw a strange dream.

He dreamed that he was in a field. Everything around was suffocated by thick fog and a steady creaking could be heard in the distance. He walked closer and saw a running carousel with horses. At first, there was nobody on it, but then he could see the figure of a woman. She sat with her back to him, face to the central pole of the attraction. She was dressed in an old-fashioned, long black dress, her curly hair carelessly fixed on the back of her head.

Then, a second woman appeared. She was dressed in a long, white nightgown. Her hair was waving, covering her face. Sam was terrified. He felt no wind but her hair was waving and her nightgown was swaying to the beat. She floated onto the carousel and sat down on one of the horses close to the center. But her head was lowered and Sam couldn't see her face.

The third figure of a woman appeared. She was moving from far away on the opposite side, jerkily approaching the carousel. Sam could already see her clothes. She was in a bright dress with large flowers. But there were no colors. Everything he saw was just black and white as if in an old movie. The figure was closer to the carousel, putting her foot on it and raising her hand to Sam, forcing him to come closer. Sam started to move forward. The woman came to meet him and in the dim lighting of the central lanterns, wrapped around a stationary pole, Sam was able to recognize her. This was the girl from the university. The one who committed suicide and determined his final choice of specialization and his whole future. He tried to call to her, but he didn't remember her name. She looked at him. Sam saw that her eyes were full of hope, but he couldn't remember her name to call her and help to break out. She stayed there for a few minutes and then gave up, sitting down on one of the horses, still looking at Sam, but with obvious disappointment.

Sam tried to approach closer to the carousel, but step by step he was not approaching an inch. The carousel remained at the same distance from him. Another figure appeared from the fog. It was not difficult for Sam to recognize her. This was Anna! He tried to shout, but his voice drowned in the sticky, wet mist. Anna climbed on the carousel and put out her hand to the woman who was sitting, facing Sam. But the woman did not see her and continued to sit indifferently. Anna went as close to her as possible and sat down on the nearby horse. Sam saw that she was smiling, her eyes glowing, and she was happy with everything that was going on. He still tried to shout to her, but to no avail.

Suddenly Sam felt someone's hand on his shoulder. He froze in surprise and fear. But summoning up courage, he turned. It was his wife. She had a wreath of wildflowers on her head. Sam remembered how she made it when they went on their last vacation during her pregnancy. She looked at him with all the tenderness and love only she was capable of when she was alive. He tried to take her hand, but couldn't reach her. He couldn't understand why she stayed so close to him. And just a moment later, he saw her going up to the carousel. She was waving to him as if saying goodbye. He again took a few steps forward, but couldn't get closer, and then another few steps—finally, he ran. But no matter how fast he tried to run, the carousel stayed the same distance from him.

The five female figures began to fade. Sam realized that at least two out of the five women were dead. But who else was there? And what was Anna doing there? He tried to scream, but his cry was lost and never reached them. He turned around, trying to figure out how to get Anna out of there. But nothing came up. All five figures disappeared. Then the carousel slowly disappeared in the fog. Sam sat down on the cold ground and hugged his head with his arms. When he opened his eyes, he saw quite a different picture.

There was Anna again. He saw her as if she were standing in a brightly lit room, looking around, not knowing where to go and what to do next. The sounds of a thunderstorm raging outside the window accompanied his dream. Thunder and the crackling of dying drops were passing their anxiety to the sleeping doctor. In his dream, he tried to call out to Anna again. He got up and took a few, confident steps forward until he hit his forehead on the glass wall that separated him from her. He tapped the glass with his fist, then stronger and stronger, but Anna didn't notice him. She turned around, staring right at the spot where Sam stood, but she looked through him as if he weren't there at all. Then she went to meet him, holding out one hand. Sam was delighted and ready to grab her hand, but Anna kept going right through him and didn't even notice him. He felt freezing cold all over his body when she went through him. Sam turned around. He saw Anna behind him. She came over to the open window, got up on the windowsill, and took a step forward. And she disappeared into the darkness. Sam heard his own deaf and helpless moan. He shuddered, got up, and looked around, not realizing where he was. The window was open. *Oh, that's why it's so cold. Hell, I have to get used to a new place*, Sam thought. He got up to close the window and almost fell down in surprise. His skin crawled. A woman sat at the dressing table. She was one of those he'd seen on the carousel. She was dressed in a black, old-fashioned dress. The woman was making up her hair, fixing it on the back of her head with studs lying on the table, gleaming in the light of the flashes. She finally fixed her hair and got up, covered her shoulders with a shawl, and approached the opened window. She sat down on the windowsill, then turned around, facing Sam for a second, but he didn't see her face. Then the woman put her legs into the open window and disappeared into the darkness. Sam stumbled backward, fell down on the bed, and finally woke up.

The window in his room was closed. There was no one at the dressing table; its top was also empty. Sam took a deep breath, turned over on his stomach and fell back asleep. The nightmares left him alone for the rest of the night.

The rain hadn't stopped and greeted the new day with a leisurely stream. Sam came out to the balcony. A breath of fresh air, already autumn air, was absolutely necessary to him. The leaves on the trees that morning were especially proud of their rich, green color, as if a belle had put on her best outfit on the day of adulthood, being proud of her beauty and youth for the last time, before it started to fade away.

The professor met Sam, as always, in the dining room. He read the newspaper, sighing and frowning.

"Good morning, Professor." Sam poured himself coffee and sat down at his usual place at the table.

"Good morning, good morning," the professor said, stretching. "Good autumn morning. The last autumn," Anri said sadly. "It sounds a bit poetic, doesn't it?"

"How are you feeling today?"

"Hmm... not bad, Doctor. I still can handle it." He threw the new paper on the table. "But could be better of course." The professor frowned. "Such a wonderful morning spoiled with the silly article about education in the style of carrot and stick. What a pity that people read all sorts of rubbish! And taking it as a guide to action! All these crazy ideas of the unprincipled hacks, deprived of talent, and angry at life itself. I doubt they have their own kids. The professor took a sip from his cup. Sam was enjoying the fresh croissant, listening to Anri attentively.

Anri continued to share his thoughts. "Why are they suppressing the minds of their children, inhibiting their wills and forcing them to act not according to their own reason and logic but according to their primitive survival instincts. That forces them to lie and dodge, avoiding another slap in the face, and helping them to get a piece of cake from the parent's table instead. These kids are capable of every wickedness and treachery for their own gain and security. They have no concept of friendship because all their friends have been betrayed and used for the carrot or just out of envy. I've met quite a few of these instances. A pathetic spectacle, you know, Doctor. I feel nothing but contempt; they are not even worth hating as this feeling is too noble for such people."

"Oh, yeah," Sam agreed. "I also had to deal with such people a couple of times. Not pleasant memories. And these rags are not the best textbook on any subject."

"It's better to stay away from such people and not to accept help even if they insist. We must always remember it is not you whom they are helping out, but they are doing it for themselves only. In order to be praised. But be careful not to owe them anything because you'll have to pay with interest. They are fairly easy to recognize. They like to brag about their heroic deeds for the sake of humanity in front of anyone willing to listen. If a person starts to share their 'good' deeds obtrusively, it is better to avoid any communication as it could cost you too much. The person who is truly benign does not consider it something special, for him it is nothing more than just a way of life. To be proud of your own way of life is the same as being proud of the ability to breathe."

Sam said nothing, only sighed deeply, and nodded in agreement. They started their breakfast. The professor tried not to attract attention, but his hands trembled more than usual.

"Has anything happened, Anri?" Sam noticed that the article was not the only thing that bothered Anri that morning.

"No, nothing special. Today we are letting Molly and Kate go to the big world. I'm always worried and a little sad when someone leaves. Although I understand that in most cases it's good. In most cases."

The professor pursed his lips slightly and looked at the doctor.

"Molly got an offer of a great position. Her new job is located in another state. We checked everything and helped to find housing and a school. They are leaving right after lunch." Anri smiled. "I'm always so attached to them, as if they are my real family. And Kate, she's such a lovely girl."

"It doesn't surprise me." Sam smiled knowingly.

Melinda glanced out the kitchen and wished them both a good morning. In a minute, she entered the dining room with a bucket of fresh-baked rolls made from a new recipe. She didn't slide back to the kitchen as usual, waiting for reviews. Anri and Sam didn't make her wait long and gave her well-deserved praise. Melinda returned to the kitchen to continue her cooking experiments.

"It's so easy sometimes to make someone happy."

"But not everybody would be satisfied with only praise. It isn't enough for everyone to be just praised."

"It's not about the praise, Sam; it's about the recognition. Praise and recognition are two different things." Anri filled his cup with hot coffee. "Sometimes it's enough to recognize something good in a person, even if they never had that thing before. Recognize and tell them about it and make them believe in it. A person will find all those good things in themselves in which they believe. But if you convince them of worthlessness and failure, even the brightest mind and God-given talent will quickly find the flaws in themselves and will wither on the vine, destroying all talents. We'll get another 'middling' who lives a mediocre life tortured by doubts and fears."

"Fear is an integral part of life. It keeps society within boundaries and often motivates some extra action." Sam followed the example of the professor and poured himself some coffee. "We are afraid of not being understood; we are afraid that someone will laugh at us; we are afraid of God knows what else. And that's kind of fine. On the other hand, fear can replace some important emotions and feelings. People often mix up fear with love. That is one of the most unpleasant things I've noticed over my practice. When people care about each other not because they love but because they are afraid to be alone. They are afraid that if they didn't care about their family members, their relatives and friends, and the entire world wouldn't give a shit about them as well. I can't call it love; for me, it's nothing more than a kind of computation. Just bare, cold calculation. Caring as if giving a loan—disgusting! I had a lot of examples among the patients, unfortunately." Sam put the cup on the table and stared at the pattern drawn with bubbles on top of a dark brown canvas framed with borders of white porcelain.

"Yes, yes, I've seen a few different families at the beginning of my practice right after university. Families who brought up their children, give them all the best they have. And when the crucial moment comes, the genuinely loving parents will give the opportunity to their child to make the choice himself. His own choice based on his own feelings, desires, and experience. They won't insist on their own unsatisfied ambitions or on what the market dictates. And in any case, they won't expect *anything* in return for the given love and care."

"The only thing is, how to recognize the crucial moment, Professor, how not to miss it once." Sam sighed.

"My dear friend." The professor smiled and looked at Sam's meaningfully, "The crucial moment comes with the first breath and lasts as long as the person is alive. Every moment is crucial! Our life consists of a daily choice, which influences all subsequent events. It is important that people have the opportunity to make that choice on their own. And here comes the main job of parents. The most important and the most difficult in my opinion." Anri cleared his throat and continued. "It is in our power to explain the different consequences. To give a chance to them to make a decision and be responsible for it in full. To give the opportunity to make a choice and proceed to give this opportunity, wisely and patiently guiding them with the participation but not the pressure. To forbid is much easier than to explain why it is not allowed, isn't it? Most likely that not from the first-time experience, but the child—a human, a *Homo sapiens*—will finally understand. In any case, he would have to be responsible for his choices every day, every hour, every minute, and he would understand the difference firsthand. No one to blame for the failure, and the next time the person would think several times before doing something or not."

Sam listened carefully, trying not to miss a single thought from the professor. He was sorry he met him so late. They were so short on time. Anri's disease had progressed. Sometimes it was hard for him to breathe, let alone speak. Coughing and choking turned into a constant wheeze. He could no longer be left alone because at any moment he could lose consciousness or curl up in unbearable pain. Sam admired the professor—such a strong will to live in spite of tormenting pain. Anri didn't want to give up, at least until he had passed the most important things over to his successor, Dr. Sam Haley. The professor was not able to smoke anymore, although this habit had been giving him the illusion of pleasure for a long time. Sam also overcame addiction out of respect for Anri. And they both stepped out to the balcony to get some fresh air instead of smoking, after the meal.

"Beautiful." Anri smiled sadly. "I feel regret that I have to leave all this beauty. Another winter will come and cover the sky with the soft clouds. Another spring will break the gray sky's sadness with the first warm rays and lovely flowers. A hot summer will replace the spring and another autumn will be rustling the leaves under our feet. But I won't be around … anymore… Time spares no one. No one can live forever. But it's okay. 'There is a time for everything, and a season for every activity under the heavens,' the Book of Ecclesiastes, the third chapter. Read at your leisure. There are some answers."

Sam couldn't find the words to say; he didn't know how to support him. And was Anri looking for support? Unlikely. He accepted his fate and was waiting in the wings, trying to get as much done as possible. Time played on the side of the enemy approaching Anri.

18

Anna stood and looked at the picture on a wall calendar. It was a picture of a field entirely covered with bright red poppies. She was always fascinated with this color, but never dared buy any red apparel or even to polish her nails this color. It seemed to her stupid and inappropriate.

She stared at the calendar for a few minutes and then tore the tape with the red square that indicated the day's date. It was Tuesday, August 23. Anna took the calendar off the wall and carefully put it into the bag along with the rest of the things she had packed already. Everything had found space in one bag. All her clothes, personal hygiene items, and some of her cherished small things. She had agreed with the property management that they would take care of the furniture, the dishes, and some home equipment Anna bought not long before. Nothing special, just a few necessary things for the kitchen: an electric pot, microwave, and toaster. Anna was doing everything slowly, thoroughly. It was obvious that she wasn't going to return to this apartment. But she had no reason to rush. She once again walked through the apartment, looked into every corner, inspected all the shelves in the bathroom and in the kitchen. No, she hadn't forgotten any of his personal belongings. Her whole life was packed into an old midsize dark-blue gym bag. And it was patiently waiting for her right next to the door.

Anna left the apartment. She closed the door and put the key under the rug, as was agreed with the landlord, who didn't even ask about the reason of her sudden decision to move out. He was not surprised by

Anna's desire to leave the furniture and kitchen equipment. Moreover, when he grimaced at the thought that he would have to dispose of all these, Anna agreed to cover any related expenses in advance. She didn't check the actual cost of the services that could be necessary, just left some cash. She did not leave her new address in case he'd need to send her money back if there were anything left over.

Anna went down the short stairs, got into her old car and turned the ignition key. She sat motionless for a few minutes. The engine rattled, poisoning the overheated day air with billowing clouds of exhaust gas. She remembered her childhood, her toys. She recalled the memory of the only one person she had ever loved. Their moments of happiness, dreams, and hopes. In spite of everything, bright and warm hopes for a better future that never happened. Memory gave her back the searing pain of loss. Tears started to flow over her face, but she calmed down quickly. In the end, everything was gone, it was all in the past, and nothing could be brought back or fixed. Nothing! It wasn't her fault, no one to blame. She made a decision. She had nothing to worry about anymore. Nothing would stop her. She finally managed to forgive. She forgave destiny and the people who were happy, who had been living in another world, inaccessible to her. She forgave all those who were luckier in life than she ever had been. And it became easier for her to breathe. She let go of her fears and doubts. She just had to wait a little more and all her nightmares would leave forever. The decision was made. The decision was final and firm. It was too late to deviate. And there was nothing behind her to escape, and no reason to do so.

The drive to the cemetery took her 20 minutes, instead of the usual 10. Anna stopped by the florist for a fresh bouquet. She counted the money left after bills and settling with the landlord and bought a huge bunch of lilies, a bottle of water, and a lighter. She had to make an effort to bring all the flowers to her car first, and then to the grave that Anna came to visit every single day, in any weather, during the last year and a half.

Amid smoothly mown lawn and faceless rows of black marble slabs, Anna put the flowers in a neat semicircle near one of them. The name on the plate was almost erased, scratched-over so much that it wasn't possible to read. There was no date of birth, only the date of death: January 28, 2014. Anna sat down beside it on the grass and tenderly stroked the gravestone, then pulled up a little closer and whispered, leaning her cheek to the marble slab, "Forgive me, forgive me everything. I am so sorry." She sat for a few minutes, then stood up, fixed the row of flowers and went back to the car. She tried in vain to contend with tears. Anna wasn't used to crying, but now everything had changed, and she didn't want to hide it anymore. She had no need to hold back; she could open up and throw out everything that had accrued over the years. Anna drove the car carefully. Tears had dried already, and she looked at the road with clear eyes. She wasn't in a hurry, but she pushed down on the gas pedal and increased her speed. However, it wasn't possible to be late to the place of her final destination.

Houses and stores floated past, but soon Anna turned onto the highway and left them all behind. The view outside the window had changed. Now she was passing the circular chain of trees nestled to the road tightly, as if they were still hoping to win an unequal battle with humans and to reclaim their previously owned land.

Anna turned off the main highway and took the exit to the camping area, which was famous because of its violent, cold river and a picturesque reservoir of the wastewater hydroelectric power station.

She parked close to the water. She actually hoped that her car would attract the attention of the police shortly. She took the bag and got out of the car, leaving on the front seat her ID and a piece of paper with neatly written words. Then she put the keys on the hood and headed to the park toward the grill area.

The campground was almost empty on a weekday. Anna chose one of the camping sites, put her bag into the fireplace hole in the ground, and lit it on fire. Anna watched quietly while the fire burned away everything related to her personal life.

She never was afraid of fire: It seemed to her something warm and harmless, unlike water. Anna hadn't learned how to swim; she was afraid of water. She didn't remember why, but for her, the water was associated with coldness and darkness. But now she felt warm while looking at the flames and thinking of nothing. She was just singing under her breath an old lullaby, which she often heard in childhood.

Sleep, my fine young baby[2]
Lullabye, a-bye.
Quietly the clear moon looks down
Into your cradle

---

[2] Michail Lermontov "Cossack Lullaby"

I will tell you stories,
I will sing you a song,
Sleep on, close your eyes,
Lullabye, a-bye.

The fire was almost out. Anna got up and slowly went toward the bridge of the main dam of the hydroelectric power station. The sun was getting ready to swap places with the rising moon and was blinding Anna with its fading rays. A light wind blew through her flowing hair. Anna was smiling. She wasn't scared, wasn't sorry for anybody. She forgave all and let go everything that had been stored in her soul for years. She finally accepted everything that happened to her as a given fate. She understood and forgave her mother and forgave the whole world. She felt easy and empty.

Anna walked to the edge of the bridge and looked around. Tears started to flow over her cheeks again. It was silent all around. The dark expanse of the water with slight ripples no longer mattered to her imagination.

She stood on the edge of the bridge. The parapet was behind her back. She stared down and whispered, "I love you so much. I miss you so much." After a few more minutes, Anna stepped forward. A few seconds later, there was a splash and spreading rings of waves. *How cold...* The last thought had flashed in her head. *Yes. That's right. It's supposed to be cold down here.*

The flow regulating valve was opened. The water fell from all the sides with a noisy, relentless flow, not leaving her a chance to change her mind, no chance to escape. A few minutes later, the stream had dried up and everything around became quiet again. The silence returned. The sun was going down, hiding

194

behind the trees. The flocks of local birds had shared space on the branches and were ready to meet the peaceful night. A rumble of a car engine disturbed the stillness. A patrol car stopped near Anna's old Ford.

The officer came over to her car and found the keys on the hood. There was not a single soul around. He did not open the vehicle, but instead he returned to his car to ascertain the name of the owner and to call for towing. Anna's car was towed to the impoundment lot. It would take some time until it would be finally opened and a piece of paper left on the front seat would be found by the cops.

19

Gina stood at the window of the wedding salon when Lucy, Matthew's mother, finally joined her.

"Oh, I'm sorry, honey, local traffic drives me crazy. It's so unlike our farm which is spacious, quiet, and clean." Lucy smiled. She looked at Gina and gently hugged her. "Come on, let's go." She was excited.

They entered the wedding salon, one of the best in the city. Bright light directed at the mannequins in white dresses and the beautiful interior had done its job. Both ladies were excited and began to look at catalogs kindly provided by the salesperson. They both rejected the offered champagne and, agreeing in tastes as always, asked for the green tea.

"When are you going to tell Matthew?" Lucy asked.

"Hmm... I don't know." Gina expected this question, but was not ready to give an answer that would satisfy Lucy.

"Just tell him. You'll see he will be happy to know. Trust me."

"Yeah." Gina felt shy. "I just don't know how to start and need to catch the right moment. He is busy now, you know, the last few days of practice, certification. A stressful time. I don't want to distract him." Gina raised her head from the catalog and met Lucy's quizzical look. "I'll tell him. Maybe even today." Gina couldn't resist Lucy's gaze.

"Great! Good girl!" That was the answer Lucy wanted to hear. "How do you like this one?" She pointed to the page with the picture of the dress with corset and fluffy skirt. "Wait, probably it would be better to find something else. No corset in your condition."

"Yes, you're right." Gina took a deep breath and slightly lowered her voice. "No corsets and no fluffy skirts."

"Oh, honey, I know. I promise we will have a masquerade ball as soon as you are able to wear a corset and fluffy skirt. I know, a wedding is an event that happens once in a lifetime. But we have a different priority now. Right?" Lucy tried to be as gentle as possible, but also pretty convincing.

"Of course. Forget about the skirt! Don't pay attention, maybe it's just the hormones playing games."

"Oh, yes! This is it! It's just started!" Lucy was beaming with joy. "Look at this one."

"Yeah, it's cute." Gina's mood began to slowly level off. "Beautiful lace."

"Handmade!" The salesperson picked up their idea. He was a handsome young man with an impressive earring in his left ear and fancy half-black, half-green framed glasses. "I'll bring you samples of different colors. We have ivory, warm dawn, and the most popular color, wintry white; it will look nice with the color of your skin." He ran to the other end of the store to get the samples.

"Yesterday I ate a whole pack of Twinkies! All 10!" Gina became sad again.

"We will get a dress with some extra space in the waist. Just in case," Lucy replied cheerfully.

"Hmm…" Gina sighed. She wasn't happy about extra space in the waist. But she could do nothing, couldn't trample nature. And each of the most significant events always has a little something that isn't perfect.

"Honey, you don't know how lucky you are." Lucy took Gina's hand and looked at her with motherly love and gratitude. "You have no idea how many women would kill to be in your place. But God is not so generous and gracious to them. Soon the hormones will calm down and you'll understand the miracle happening within you."

Gina smiled. Of course she had a full understanding of everything that happened to her and she was infinitely happy. But the hormones during this period were not predictable—they mock the mood, using their temporal authority. The salesman came back with the promised samples of lace and a bunch of different fabrics. Lucy and Gina started seriously discussing all the details of her future wedding dress.

The same day, in the late evening, Gina got herself together and finally announced the news to her fiancé. Matthew's knees buckled; he was surprised and delighted and even shed tears of happiness. They decided they would not postpone the wedding, but would have to skip the honeymoon trip. Better not to tempt fate and not to risk anything. Matthew insisted on Gina's immediate move to his place, and no one cared that her rent was paid until the end of autumn. Now he more than ever wanted to be continuously next to her, to take care of her, fulfill her every whim. Matthew was that king of a husband Gina dreamed about. And Matthew thought that he was so lucky to meet Gina; he adored his bride. There was no secret about their relationship. They never had obtuse discussions or unbridled passion. They just had met "the right person," as if both been made for each other. They had waited for each other, never settling for less.

A happy life was waiting for them. A beautiful, healthy child just six months later (Gina was already in the third month of her pregnancy). A great success for Matthew's projects and a true harmony. They were falling asleep and waking up perfectly happy, regardless of the season and the weather outside. Both learned the way to find beauty in everyday routines and worries. Every difficulty they were faced with—and there many, as any other family experiences—drew them together. Gina would blossom after the baby was born. She would find her true destiny in motherhood and become a wonderful mother and a happy wife.

20

The Five Stars archive was given a separate building not far from the main gate of the clinic. The thick walls with firmly concreted windows carefully kept all the secrets of many families away from the rest of the world behind the iron door with a massive, ingenious lock. Only Anri, Isabelle, and Lola had access to the archive—people who never would betray the stories of their patients. It was difficult for the professor to cope with the disobedient lock, which was rusted in some places. Sam offered his help, and Anri gratefully accepted his offer and walked away. Sam successfully turned the key, but the lock did not open. The doctor saw the letters on the nine wheels and realized it was necessary to set the words on each wheel. He looked at the professor.

Anri smiled and declared, "When halfway through the journey of our life I found that I was in a gloomy wood, because the path which led aright was lost[3]."

"Nine wheels, nine guardians, pretty simple."

The professor stood and smiled, pleased with himself. It was his idea to encrypt the entrance to the archive. Of course, the standard digital code would be enough, but Anri wanted to make the cipher unusual.

"I got it. Hmm, quite symbolic."

"Thank you, I knew you'd like it."

"I don't remember all nine of the guardians, to be honest."

"Don't worry, I am still here to help."

"And I don't quite understand how to enter the words."

"Oh, it's simple." The professor got closer. "Here, you see numbers and a little arrow. Push the number one after another and bring each word's letters

---

[3] Dante Alighieri, The Divine Comedy "Inferno 1"

to line up with the arrow alternately wheel by wheel. And the lock will open."

"Okay, the first, Charon." Sam cautiously turned the first wheel, aligning the desired letter to the arrow. As soon as the last letter reached the arrow, he heard the distinctive click.

"Minos." A click again. "Cerberus, Plutus, Phlegyas."

Sam turned to the professor with a questioning look.

"Just Furies, didn't want to hurt either one, so I decided to depersonalize them," Anri replied in a guilty tone.

"Oh, okay. The Furies, then, the Minotaur, now Geryon." Click by click, the lock was confirming the correctness of Sam's answers. For the last wheel, Sam hesitated, and again turned his questioning gaze to the professor.

"Lucifer. I decided that he is a true guardian of the ninth circle. Forgive me this liberty in interpretation." Anri showed a guilty smile again.

Sam put in the final name-code and the lock finally gave up. He pulled the heavy ring that served as the door handle and the door opened. Sam stopped and waited for Anri.

"It is important to make sure that the data won't ever fall into the wrong hands. It can ruin people's lives. Many of our guests are from rich and famous families. Ridiculous—it would seem that they have everything to live a happy life." Anri turned on the light, a single, dim lamp close to the ceiling of the vestibule. "The disease overtakes one of them first."

He got a bunch of keys, opened a lattice door, and stepped forward.

"I am not surprised." Sam followed the professor. "Usually, they grow apart from the serious stress. They always have something to eat, something to wear, and it is always warm and safe around. Although many such families have a risk of mental disorders since infancy. Kids spend most of their time with nannies and it's not always the same person. The babysitters often change. And the main guarantor of a stable psyche of a child, his mother, she often saves her body and beauty, tries to sleep enough and sees the baby for a couple of hours a day when the child is fed, dressed, and not screaming. They are saying they would step up to the pressures of raising their own children after they grow up a bit. They are really thinking that children do not understand who is taking care of them, who feeds them, gives them baths and gets up at night to calm down their nightmares, even though the important part of mental stability is formed in early infancy. The connection between the child and the parent is interrupted. and the child feels abandoned, no matter how much gold is embedded in his rattle and what brand his clothes are. Even the most kind and attentive babysitter can never replace a mother, no matter how carefully they do their job, no matter how much they get paid for it."

Sam stared at one point and quietly continued.

"No one can replace a mother. No matter how good the man is, no matter how cared for; there is something instinctive, something on an animal level. Whatever the mother may be, she is best for her child.

At least in early childhood, this is the most common comprehension."

"I can't disagree with you, Sam, although someone else can step in sometimes—it all depends on the individual."

Anri turned on the light; this time bright fluorescent lights lit the room. A wide room with rows of racks with neatly lined-up folders in alphabetical order. On each shelf was a tablet with an indicated diagnosis.

"Whatever the conditions of life, the main thing is that a mentally healthy parent is nearby and taking care of the baby as good as she can. And no matter how old and ugly the walls are that surround their little world. The main thing is that love reigns in this little world. Certainly, the difficult conditions of life with the right attitude of wise parents will help the child grow strong, ready to overcome the difficulties. And become the person who will not break at the first failure or difficult situation. But we are talking about mentally healthy people, of course. A sick man with any way of life would not cooperate without professional medical assistance."

"Well, the first difficulty is to reach an unhealthy person and try to persuade him to accept help. They rarely come on their own. Too rare."

"I regret that you are right. Some of our guests came to us too late. You saw the patients of Five Stars, but their lives could have turned out differently."

The professor came to the next lattice door, found the right key, and opened it. He gestured for Sam to follow him. "But the worst thing, my friend, is when signs of the disease are not visible to anyone. Instead the unhealthy mother looks caring to everyone, covering all her actions with supposedly good things for a child. Have you ever heard about the Dead Mother complex?"

"I'm, I'm not really sure, I might have read, but…" Sam tried to remember, but to no avail.

"Andre Green was the first who looked into this matter deeply." Anri coughed and paused for a few seconds, then continued. "But there is a worse, much scarier side of this syndrome. We call it the phenomenon of the Dead Killing Mother Syndrome. And unfortunately, it's common and not easy recognizable. You'll have plenty of time to study numerous ailments." The professor waved at the countless shelves with folders of all the guests' cases.

"The dead killing mother syndrome." Professor went to the rack with tens of folders on each row. "Impressive isn't it? These are only the crumbs, those who gave vent to their illness and went to extremes."

There were some old folders and a lot of new, with the smell of fresh ink, with the smell of fresh pain and suffering. Anri continued after a short pause. "Usually, it all starts with the little things. The mothers show cruelty to the children, emotional rejection, neglect; the mothers humiliate their children by all known methods. But the fact is that women suffering from this disorder create the impression of caring mothers with unconditional love, so it's hard to recognize the disease, especially if the woman is alone and has no one to watch her."

Anri took a few folders from the shelf and passed them to Sam. "A lot of mothers suffer from this disorder. A special group at risk are the single mothers.

No one to help cope with the emotional accompaniments of pregnancy and childbirth. No one to support them in a time of postpartum physical pain and fatigue. Here are some cases, some of the most striking." Anri pointed to the folders he just gave to Sam "And so, against this background, often postpartum depression develops, and then it could turn into the dead killing mother syndrome. It always goes along with hidden hatred for the child because the woman cannot admit to herself that she hates her child. She doesn't want to understand that it's just a disease that must be treated accordingly. But she would never ask for help! She was raised the same way, and she's a mother and needs to follow her idea of motherhood. And so often this idea appears distorted beyond recognition, disfigured by the cult of motherhood, stupidity, and ignorance. And we are getting a generation of crippled, unfortunate people. One generation after another."

Sam opened the first folder and read the diagnosis and description of the dead killing mother syndrome, progressive state, shown with some unconscious aggressive impulses, in the form of "accidental misconceptions." The child several times "accidentally" fell out of bed and the changing table, mother a few times "accidentally" hit the wall with the baby's head. According to the woman, she didn't mean to hurt him; they all were accidents. The child was subjected to intensive treatment for a severe concussion four times. Each concussion was the result of the accidental, incautious acts of the mother.

Sam wondered. He remembered when he was a child he watched their neighbor and her child. There were always some kind of small household accidents happening to her child. Sam's aunt always felt pity for her. And the neighbor lady then always shouted with tears, pretending she felt sorry for her poor little son. She was always complaining about the accidents, saying something like "he wriggled and fell out of my hands." A couple of times in his memory, she complained that he "crawled under her arm accidentally when she was cooking dinner, and cut himself," thereby excusing the wound on her child's body. No one ever dared to accuse her of child abuse. And she created the impression of a kind, caring mother, always so worried about what had happened. She cried that she was destined to be alone because she was a good mother and it was her choice, and with men you never knew if they were a tyrant, and she wouldn't allow anyone to hurt her child. *Anyone, except, of course, herself,* Sam thought when he understood that she was sick all along. Sam remembered that he always felt jealous of this kid. The neighbor child seemed so cared for. His mother never left him for a long time and didn't trust him to anyone. Sam always dreamed that his mother was nearby. He continued to read a short description of the syndrome. "A woman persecuted by destructive killing impulses in the form of unpredictable outbursts of anger, rage, and cruelty to her own child. These outbreaks then are presented as profound care and love."

The professor interrupted his thoughts. Anri coughed heavily. Sam remembered one case that he read about when he was studying at the university.

"Professor, you may have heard about the case when the mother chained her daughter to the bed and kept her locked up in her room for 20 years just to keep her away from the guy she was supposed to marry. The mother thought he didn't deserve to marry her daughter. When the truth was found out, the girl was rescued. She was exhausted, suffered from sores all over her body. No one took care of her properly, while her mother was sure she was doing the right thing, saving her daughter from the villain who could ruin the life of her beloved child. Could that be considered a hyper-progressive condition, of course with hints of schizophrenia?"

"I think it could be, although it is more like schizophrenia with hints of the syndrome. Most often, this syndrome shows itself in a different way. For example, I can describe one of the forms, which is quite common and looks like a manifestation of the maternal instinct." Anri leaned over the wall.

It was hard for him to stand for a long time as well as to speak. But he had to catch every single moment and give away as much as he could. Time was playing against him. He didn't show a hint of being tired and continued. "Pay attention to the mothers who are concerned about the health of their children. These mothers are interested in illness of a child, his failure. They are compassionate and full of care if something bad happens to a child. They spend a lot of care and energy bringing attention to bad things. And they always make dire predictions about the future of their children. They always have a huge worry about the child, pretending they know for sure that something bad will happen to the kid. God forbid the kid gets sick, falls off the slide, or is hit by a car, and this list of possibilities is endless, it all depends on the imagination of each individual mother."

Anri tried to explain to Sam, "Let's imagine that I am a mommy of a girl, and I am constantly worrying for her, what if she'd be raped. Or, I'm scared all the time; I'm afraid that anything bad will happen, what if she grows up and becomes a drug addict. This kind of constant fears is killing all possible good emotions, programming the child for failure and fair against everything, again, all depends on individual, but it always works the same way."

Emotions never left Anri. He, as always, transmitted everything through his own soul.

The professor paused for a little, caught his breath and continued. "Such mothers turn blind eyes, staying indifferent to any of the good changes and do not react to the joy of a child. In adulthood, the children of these mothers say they can felt genuine care, love, and interest from their mother only when something bad happened to them. And when everything was fine, they had a feeling that Mommy was not happy at all, and even seemed disappointed that nothing bad had happened. The nightmares of these mothers are always full of sickness, death, blood, and corpses. Most of them don't cause visible physical damage to the children through their behavior, but gradually and systematically, they suppress in them the joy of life and confidence, faith in development, faith in life. And in the end, they infect them with their own 'lethality.' The child begins to be afraid of life, and in the end, reaches for death." Sweat popped out on the professor's face. He spoke so emotionally that Sam felt as if he were one of the mothers who was suffering from the syndrome.

"Forgive me my emotions, Sam; it's painful for me. We can't help these poor little ones. They have to grow slowly, dying from the inside, maintaining silence. The dead silence."

"Silence." Sam nodded few times. "And they keep this dead silence all through life, pretending everything is okay, never seeking help. How hard is it to allow yourself to realize that you need help, Professor? It must be impossible to admit that your mom is the cause of your loneliness and never-ending pain. Of course, she always took so much care." His smile was sad, hopeless.

"We are slowly but surely killing humanity with our own hands, by killing our own children in one way or another. Not much to expect in the future. But if we can save one suffering soul, we do not live in vain, and all this," Anri swept his eyes around, "is not in vain. You'll see, it's not in vain."

Anri motioned Sam to follow him, again pulled out a bunch of keys and rattled it in search of the right one. This time he quickly found the needed one and opened the next barred door.

"On these shelves, you'll find the answers to all your questions. Many of these 'fates' have already left this world. Some on their own will." Anri leaned against the wall, loudly coughed, and for a moment, was lost in space. Sam jumped to him and managed to keep him on his feet, not letting the professor fall down. Sam quickly took pills out of the right pocket of the professor's jacket and put one into his mouth. Anri swallowed the pill immediately. They stood like that for a few minutes. The spasm decreased slowly. The drug began to work. The professor felt better. He straightened up but still stood leaning on the wall.

"I always forget the time of my next pill. Sorry that I scared you, Sam."

Sam didn't say anything, just lifted up the corners of his mouth, trying to fake a smile. There was nothing to smile about, but Anri was not discouraged. He pulled away from the wall and unsteadily walked to the next door. The keys jingled and another door opened, baring all secrets of the Five Stars' guests. The professor walked over to the first rack on his way, then put his hand into the opened drawer with folders, and pulled out a random case.

"I remember each of them. My memory is my enemy and my friend at once." Without looking at the folder, he handed it to Sam.

"Tell me the name, Sam, and I'll tell you the entire history of the disease, everything to the smallest detail, no, better to say, I'll tell you the story of another life."

Sam realized that Anri was trying to convey to him how it was important to evince the utmost participation in the fate of each guest, how it was important to feel their pain in order to find a way out, to find an individual door to salvation. Sam opened folder, looked at the first page and froze. His eyes widened, his mouth opened slightly, and he turned pale.

"Anna!" Sam reeled. He felt dizzy.

"Anna?" Anri repeated with doubt, went to the doctor, and looked into the folder. "Oh, Anna. No, this is not Anna. This is her mother—Maria."

Sam felt as if his head was spinning. The lump had stuck in his throat and his breathing was fast and heavy.

"Sam, are you okay? What's wrong with you?" Anri looked at Sam with worry. He had never seen Sam in a state of shock. "Sam." The professor lightly slapped the doctor on the cheek. Sam came around and raised his eyes from the photo on the first page of the folder and stared at the professor. Dr. Haley could not utter a word.

"This is Maria." Anri pointed to the photo on the opened folder, which Sam held in his hands. "She had a daughter—Anna. Do you know Anna, Sam?"

"Yes, Anna." Sam 's composure gradually began to return to him, and he tried to get himself together. "Yes, she is … my…" Sam paused. He couldn't find the right word to explain who Anna was to him. "Remember I told you about the girl. And I was looking for you to meet her. She needs help. She and her baby. I mean. That was her I was talking about."

"Yes, I remember now. I think you said postpartum depression with a possible admixture of sluggish schizophrenia, but—"

"Anri, she disappeared." Sam's voice was breaking.

"Who?" Professor couldn't catch Sam's mind.

"Anna. She disappeared." Sam was trying to speak calmly, but his voice wasn't obeying.

"What do you mean, disappeared?" Anri was confused.

"She canceled our sessions, quit her job, and her phone is off. I can't find her. I was going to ask you to help me find her. But I couldn't find the right moment. My intuition… I feel that she's in trouble." Sam was flustered again; he remembered last night's dream.

"Of course, sure, Sam. Don't worry. I'll call the officer as soon as we get out of here. There's no network connection here."

"She came to me last time as usual a couple weeks ago. And I did not understand what happened to her, if she had told the truth or… I never really understood her, probably didn't understand her at all. She, her child…"

"Child? My friend, what child are you talking about?" The professor frowned.

"Her child. She never said a name or gender. But she talked about the baby, about screaming that drove her crazy every night. She couldn't handle it. I think she is harming her child. I mean … well … she was saying such things… I am not sure." Sam finally got lost in his own thoughts and guesses.

"Anna never had children. Even if she'd want to have a baby, she can't have children."

"But…" Sam turned pale.

"We both need fresh air. Come on, Sam. Let's sit on a bench outside. Let's go outside. I'll tell you her story if you want."

"Yes, sure."

They quickly went outside. Anri left all the opened doors as they were. Sam sat on the bench, as Anri headed to the golf cart. He pulled out from under the driver's seat a stashed pack of cigarettes and then returned to Sam and offered him one.

"Thank you." Sam took the cigarette with trembling hands and lit it. He took a deep puff and everything swam in his eyes. Nicotine intoxication hit him, and he calmed down a bit.

"This photo." Anri took the folder from Sam's trembling hands, opened it, and pointed to a photo of woman on the first page. "This is Maria—Anna's mother. They look similar as two peas. Maybe this is what at some point saved Anna's life. I mean the fact that she doesn't look like her father, but is the spitting image of Maria. Later, Anna changed her hair color to blond. That was the only difference between them. Maria had hair a ripe chestnut color. They looked like two sisters at one point. Only the age and the hair color were different. You can find a full description of Maria's diagnosis here. And there's also some information about Anna. Poor girl. I'll never forget the look in her eyes, especially the one she gave me in our first meeting."

Anri lit a cigarette too. He coughed heavily, but didn't stop smoking.

The professor looked at the doctor. Sam sat in silence with his head bowed, staring at one point. The cigarette between the fingers of his right hand was slowly smoldering, turning its paper and tobacco to ash. The last hope of Sam that Anna still had a chance was turning to ash along with the cigarette. Anri caught his breath and continued.

"Despite everything, Anna kept her inner strength. And always, always this stony, heavy gaze of a person who had to fight for existence from the first breath. The gaze of a human who was doomed to suffer from the hands of her own mother. But despite all the harm, Anna loved her mother. She was trying to forgive her, was trying to understand why she couldn't just love her. Why she gave up so easily and didn't choose to fight for herself. And Anna's disease, that she

212

accidentally got in childhood, I mean HIV. She did her best and fought, but it seemed that the disease had troubled her the least. The most important thing for her was to understand her mother. To forgive her. She didn't manage it. At least not here."

"She did. She managed it." A tear slowly slid at Sam's cheek. He didn't try to hide it. He didn't wipe it away. He didn't care about anything that was happening in the world at that moment. Anything except Anna and her story.

"Anna decided to leave as soon as her mother died. Maria committed suicide in front of her daughter. We still don't know what happened between them. That day, Anna, as always, came to visit her; everything was as usual. Then, the nurse who was on duty heard the sound of broken glass and a thud. Maria broke the window with a chair and jumped through it. Since that accident, we put bars on the windows in the Five Stars building and had all the furniture bolted to the floor. The nurse quickly ran to the fourth floor and when she entered the room, Anna stood in the middle and held the cup of tea in her hands. She just stood there and drank tea, looked so calm, as if nothing happened." Anri lit another cigarette. "I immediately noticed a dramatic change in her behavior. She went deep into herself, stopped reacting to the things that usually pleased her. I think she just lost the last hope. She didn't care about anything else anymore. After a few days, Anna left. I couldn't force her to stay, despite the depression and sickness. I couldn't keep her here. She was only a guest, and you know our rules. The only thing she asked for was to bury her mother at one of the city cemeteries. She wanted to visit her grave as often as possible. And it's too far to drive here. Of course, I could not say no to her. And so, we did." The professor extinguished the cigarette and took a deep breath.

Sam took a pack and continued to smoke one cigarette after another. Tears flowed down his cheeks. Anri could understand Sam's feelings, but couldn't help.

"She would never hurt anyone. She was always a warm-hearted girl, in spite of everything, kind. She just didn't know how to express her emotions, either good or bad. She always kept everything inside. And her stony, heavy gaze…" These last words Anri said almost in a whisper.

"She came to me seeking help. I didn't understand her. I was drowning in my own stuff, pretending to know what was happening to her. Now I know. Now I understand it. But it's too late." Sam was speaking slowly and in a low voice. The tears on his face dried. "She talked about the scream, now I know, that was her scream. She could not calm herself out of the scream, and I didn't help her. I thought she was talking about the baby, and she tried to explain to me, but I didn't hear he." The tears came back. "Didn't want to hear … she was saying, 'I am child. I am baby.' She repeated it again and again, and I didn't hear. I didn't realize that she was the baby who was harmed. She was the one who suffered. She was just recalling her memory, trying to figure out how to relieve the pain; she was talking all this time about herself. The poor 'killed' child. Oh God, how deaf I was to her!" Sam felt aching pain as if something blunt was tearing his chest from the inside but couldn't break through.

214

He cried—silently, helplessly cried. He understood that he would never see Anna again. He knew the only thing that kept her in this world finally let her go. In their last meeting, Anna said she felt free. She could neither understand nor forgive her mother, but infinitely loved her anyway and finally something had changed, and she managed to accept all that happened to her just as fact. She was free from the heavy, painful weight she was trailing through her whole life. She made a decision, made her choice.

The professor sat beside Sam silently. He didn't say a word either to comfort him or to support him. He knew Sam must go through it himself, open his eyes wider, and realize the things he wouldn't be able to realize otherwise. Anri remembered himself. The other himself, young and ambitious, when he first was confronted with his own desperate helplessness, when he for the first time was faced with the dead silence. It was a long time ago, and he had changed since then. He tried not to let that happen. But. There is always a *but*, and people make their own decisions, make their own choices, at the crucial moment...

> *"Wherefore I praised the dead which are already dead: more than the living which are yet alive. But better than both is the one who has never been born, who has not seen the evil that is done under the sun"*

> — Ecclesiastes, 4:2 and 3